THE **BOY** CHRONICLES

"Set YOURSELF Free"

-Mike Spears

Meet The Author

Mike Spears, the true definition of multi-talented. Coming from the small impoverished community of Pembroke, Illinois has seasoned Mike with a keen humble spirit that's destined for success. Landing a major recording contract with Universal Music Group, Mike has proven himself as a singer/ songwriter. Leading him to perform and appear on major networks like; MTV, BET, VH1, and FOX. After a few singles failing to chart, and a fully un-released album Mike found himself at odds with life and the music business. Taking a hiatus from the music business to literally travel around world, Mike took out time to write about his life and experiences as a recording artist in his first book titled *Reason Why I Sing*. Now returning to the literary world with his second effort, "The Boy X Chronicles", Mike hopes to tell a series of stories that will bring more perspective and awareness to the "gay lifestyle" and HIV/AIDS.

WARNING

Though some of this work is based on real life events and situations, it is a work of fiction. Names, characters, places and incidents are either the product of the author's imagination or are used fictitiously, and any resemblance to actual persons, living or dead, business establishments, events or locales is entirely coincidental.

-Spearit Publishing

THE BOY CHRONICLES

The Boy X Chronicles

Table of Contents

Acknowledgements

ALAN KLINE

THE BOY CHRONICLES

Birthday: March 25
Sign: Aries
Occupation: Photographer
Highest Education: Master Degree in Fine Arts and Photography
Personality Type: Ambitious, Hopeless Romantic, People Pleaser

ALAN

Oh my God, I can't believe this. How could something like this happen to me? I was so careful with everything in my life. Just one night of vulnerability led me here, in this cold place. Now I'm just another statistic. I'm part of the club I once talked so much about. Just to hear the words, "You Are HIV positive", made me die a million times. I lost all the breath out of my body. My lungs fell in a state of shock, so I couldn't grab the air to breathe. My blood rushed to the center of the Earth as my heart began to beat the cold blood of death. To keep my body from hyperventilating, my stomach had set itself on fire as my bones had clasped upon themselves. I slipped from the chair where I was sitting onto the floor. The nurse quickly rushed to my side to console me. I tried to get myself up but my body wasn't responding to my minds commands. My tears are coming so fast that they are jammed in my tear ducts. After about ten straight minutes of me just completely breaking down, the nurse was able to get me to calm down.

She rubbed my back and asked me, if I knew who I may have gotten this disease from.

Being stuck with a disease that I felt only irresponsible people got, I couldn't tell her the truth. To be honest, I don't know who he was but I told the nurse I did. She offered to contact him and bring him in for testing, but I told her that I will contact him myself. I can't help but replay that night over and over in my head. I know I had a lot to drink and I was a bit too friendly that night but no, this could not have happened to me. I don't even remember his name. Hell, I barely remember how he looked. I could probably walk right past him and not know who he was. I know I allowed him to follow me back to my apartment and we had sex. I couldn't remember if we used a condom or not...

After a while of consoling me, the nurse asked me if I was suicidal. I told her no, not at all. However, in my mind, I knew if I had to die, then somebody else was going to die with me. I was furious and wanted to find this snake that had did this to me. I didn't want to just find him to confront him, no, I wanted him dead...

ALAN I:

I only went out that night because I had just broke up with Lance. Lance and I have been together for three and a half years. People that we mutually knew in Atlanta loved us together. People called us "Cookies n Crème" because I was light skinned and he was a darker brown complexion than I. He was a 6'2 underwear and runway model that traveled all around the world for work. I'm a 5'9 photographer that also worked as Lance's assistant on the side. I had actually met him during a shoot he did for GQ magazine. At that time, I worked as the assistant to the photographer of that particular shoot. We hit it off right away. Since the day we had met, we only spent a total of nine days, 19 hours and about 22 minutes apart. We ate, slept, talked, walked, laughed, and danced together. We were inseparable. Whenever we both were in between work, we would shack up in a two bedroom condo that we shared in Marietta, Georgia.

After about our two and a half year mark in our relationship, things changed between Lance and me. He decided that I should no longer be his assistant. He felt like we were spending way too much time together and he needed his space from "us" sometimes. Though it hurt that he felt this way, I skeptically agreed. Just as any relationship the beginning seems to be the best part. That's when you're just learning each other and you're infatuated by each other's every move.

In the beginning, he told me that he wanted me around all the time and that's where we got the idea for me to be his assistant. Being Lance's assistant wasn't an easy task, especially when I have to sit back and watch him entertain his "fans". It seemed like everywhere we went some chick was stopping him to tell him how "fine" he was. And to watch other gay guys flirt with him was the worse. He never wanted to seem like an "ass hole" so he always played it nice with them, even when they would touch all over his body. I really felt like he should have stopped them, out of respect for me. Deep down I did understand him not wanting to come off as a jerk. I guess the other side of me wanted to see Lance take a stand for me. Just something like him putting someone in their place, because of something they did made me feel uncomfortable, would make me feel like he really cared for my feelings. But I admit at times it made me feel extremely insecure. My insecurity ignited a trait of jealously that no human should be born with. In my mind Lance was mine and I didn't want to share him with the world, regardless of his occupation.

After we decided that I would no longer be his assistant our relationship expectedly changed. He went ahead and hired another assistant in which was a beautiful young lady by the name Amanda. Amanda was bi-racial; she was mixed with African American and Cuban. She had long jet black hair; I always told her she reminded me of Pocahontas. Amanda was a nice girl. She would always come to our place and spend time with the both of us. We all would go out to the night clubs together. When she was dumped and put out by her boyfriend, we took her in. Since we did have an extra bedroom, we didn't mind her staying with us because she loved to clean and we trusted her. Whenever Lance had to fly over seas for a job, she would go with him. Since I was no longer his assistant, I was able to focus on my own photography but our relationship suffered.

We went from communicating all day to not at all. Even when he was back at home in Georgia we didn't speak much. We slept in the same bed and would not touch each other. I knew something was wrong. If there's one thing Lance wanted at night, it was a piece of me. Since we've spent days apart and him not even trying to make a move on me, I knew he must have been having sex with another guy. Just the thought of him touching someone else made my heart cringe. I would feel like Jean Gray from the X-Men, I wanted to torch everything in sight. I would have hot flashes when I thought of the possibility of him cheating.

For over two months Lance and I haven't been intimate with each other. Whenever I did try to make a move on him he would always say he's really tired. There was a time when we would have sex about two times every day. Even on our busiest days we found time to fool around. I wasn't sure what I could do to get him to be the same person I fell in love with. I didn't want to just give up on us and possibly find someone else. I couldn't imagine myself with anyone else but him. I decided to change my hair a bit from the curly high top to a low even cut. I thought maybe my hair was turning him off. I even started to spend more time in the gym. Even though I was in great shape; I just thought maybe I wasn't good enough for him. I was going crazy trying to figure him out.

I thought I had my opportunity to rekindle our relationship when he came down with a really bad cold. Since he was ill, I cancelled all my photography appointments to be home with him. I cooked for him and made sure he had all he needed to feel better. I wanted to prove to him that I was the one he needed. He seemed to be extremely appreciative of me helping him while he was sick.

One night in my attempt to rekindle the "romanticism" in our relationship, I ran him some bath water. I walked him to the tub where I had lit candles and even had glasses of red wine waiting. I slowly washed him as he grabbed my hand and kissed it. I fell in love with him all over again. That small kiss on the hand drove my mind through a vortex of old memories we shared. He grabbed the back of my head, pulled my face to his and gave me the most passionate kiss I had ever felt. With no care, I climbed in the tub fully clothed. I was determined to rescue our love from drowning. I kissed him as if he had just got back from a world war. He pulled my wet t-shirt off and softly clinched his teeth into my neck. The hot exhaled air from his nostrils on the back of my neck melted my heart every time. I could have died a good death just feeling his fingers running down my lower back removing my underwear and sweat pants in one motion. My heart had begun to race and my breath was shortening as tears streamed down my face. He licked and kissed every tear away while repeating, "I'm sorry." I could care less what he had done at that point because this moment made it all worth it. We made love once again and I just knew then that our love was saved.

ALAN II:

The next day I had a photo shoot with a new marketing company that lasted eleven hours, from 10am to 9pm. I was extremely exhausted from working but after last night my energy for life was restored. Since modeling work had slowed down for Lance, I didn't mind doing the extra mile of working. I knew what I was doing was going to benefit me and my love. I arrived home that night around 10:15pm, excited to see Lance. When I walked in the door, I was a bit disturbed to find Lance lying on the sofa with his feet on Amanda's lap. I could tell that I had walked in on something that wasn't appropriate by how they were acting. They both seemed suspiciously quiet. She seemed as if she could have just been massaging his feet. I know that he had been sick, but not to the point where she should be massaging his feet. I knew they were very close but definitely not that close. The thing that really burned my heart was that; he was only wearing underwear. My first instinct was to just totally flip out. I wanted to punch both of them through the heart so they could physically feel what I felt. Since she was fully clothed, I didn't want to over react. I said hello to the two of them and walked fast and hard to my room. I felt that warm sensation of anger rush through my veins. Lance asked me from that other room how was work and I told him it was good. I answered so quickly and direct that I felt like I was a robot. I'm sure by the way I said it he could tell that something was wrong with me. Amanda came to my room trying to make small talk, asking me about my photo shoot. If she only knew how much I wanted to grab her by her long pretty hair and drag her through this entire condo, she wouldn't have bothered me. She seemed a bit nervous which made me even more suspicious of her now. I never thought for a second that Lance and Amanda could have had interest in each other. We treated Amanda like a sister; the thought of them hooking up is a bit disturbing. Lance has never expressed to me that he had an interest in women anyways. I thought maybe I was thinking too hard about the whole situation. Amanda would never do anything like that to hurt me.

When Lance came to bed that night I attempted to cuddle with him but he didn't react. I thought we were getting back to us after last night but no. I felt like last night was a fairy tale built with false hopes. I wasn't sure what was on his mind.

The next morning I woke up facing the window. Normally I would have woken up facing the opposite direction lying on Lance's chest. The sun reigned through the blinds onto my face and the still quietness of nothingness ringed at a high pitch in my ears. I rolled over to find that Lance was not there. I wasn't surprised he wasn't lying in bed with me. I figured that he may have been in the living room watching TV. I went to the bathroom that's connected to our room to find a letter taped to the mirror that read,

"Alan, I just can't live like this anymore. I'm leaving and I will not return. There's is no need to call me because I have changed my number. Bye."

I snatched the letter from the window, clenched it close to my heart as I fell to my knees in tears. I couldn't believe what I just read and how poorly written it was. We had been together too long and been through too much for him to just up and leave me like this. He didn't even have the balls or just the decency to talk to me. This condo is in both of our names. I was hoping maybe he wasn't this foolish and just wanted to blow off some steam. I got myself together quickly and rushed to the closet to see that he didn't take a lot of his things. I felt confident that he'll be back. I went to Amanda's room to find that all of her belongings were gone. There was no sign of her either. I was in total disbelief I swear I thought I was dreaming. I tried to call Amanda's cell phone but I didn't get an answer. I called over and over and left messages each time I called. I wonder if my suspicion of Amanda and Lance was true. How long has this been going on?

Being so hurt I had to call my best friend Tony. I knew that he could say the right things to help me cope with what was going on. Tony is a very loud and flamboyant type of guy. He watches all types of reality TV shows and he acts just like the characters on those shows. He knows all the latest lingo and always looking for the perfect opportunity to use them. He loves to "read" people, meaning he loves telling people the truth about themselves. Or at least what he thinks their truth may be. He's extremely straight forward and not to be toyed with, meaning he loves to fight. I met Tony when I first moved to Atlanta about six years ago at Six Flags. At the time we both had a little thing for each other but we soon discovered that we were better off as friends.

I decided to go over to Tony's place just to get out of the house. Tony tells me that he never really liked Lance any ways. Just as a friend would do, he tells me everything that I need to hear to feel empowered about this situation. I really felt lost in this situation because everything seemed so right the other night. Tony wants to drive around Atlanta and find him and Amanda and "whoop their asses", as he loves to say. Though I'm extremely hurt I can't find it in my heart to do harm to Lance, but Amanda would be a different story. I'm not the type of guy to fight a chick but hearing Tony definitely ignited the devious fire within me.

Tony made me realize all the sacrifices that I've made to be with Lance. I passed up several great paying contracts with Major Advertising Firms in New York and Los Angeles to stay close to Lance. Lance suggested that if I truly believed in him and wanted to be with him then I would pass on those offers. He always reassured me that he would work and make the money for the both of us, but of course, this was back then when I was his assistant. Even though I've done financially well in Atlanta and racked in a few prestigious photography awards, I always wondered how things would have been if I had took those contracts.

To get me to smile, Tony had the nerve to play "Not Gon' Cry" by Mary J Blige, and he sings "three in a half years of sacrifice, besides the kids I have nothing to show." Even though we didn't have kids we were definitely thinking about adopting after we got married. I really love Tony for being a great friend. Though I was hurting over Lance's disappearing act, it felt good to laugh.

Later that night I went home and cried for almost two hours straight. I cried so much that I had a head ache. I even tried to call Lances phone in which his voicemail did pick up. At least he didn't change his number, yet. Maybe he was planning to change it soon. I called constantly and left messages asking him to please talk to me. Feeling so depressed I thought of committing suicide thinking hopefully he'd find out and come running to my side. I haven't had these suicidal thoughts since high school. The feeling of loneliness and no one that I could relate to made me feel dead inside. I much rather be dead than to feel the pain I was feeling.

ALAN III:

After feeling sorry for myself, I decided that I should go out to a club to just be around some other people. I called Tony and asked if he'd like to go out with me. He couldn't go because he had to get up for work the next morning. I decided to go alone to a gay night club called "Tricks". I've never went out to any night club alone, but desperate times call for desperate measures. "Tricks" was a very upscale type of night club. Some of Atlanta's more dignified gay men came to this club. Lance and I would come here every now and then, whenever we were in town.

Walking into the club alone made me feel just that, "alone". The music was pumping loud with the dance floor full of people. I'm not the dancing type so I made my way to the bar. I was hoping that I could possibly get a good conversation started with anyone who felt sorry enough to talk to me. When I made my way to the bar I finally got the bartender's attention and ordered a double of "Rum and Coke". The bartender was very attractive white guy that I had never seen before. I tried to small talk and make eye contact with him to let him know that I was interested but he didn't seem to pay it any mind. After about three drinks I knew I was past tipsy but I was enjoying watching all the others dance and have a good time.

Out of nowhere I was approached by a guy who stood directly behind me, put both his hands on my shoulders and whispered, "Can I get you a drink". I smiled and turned around slowly. I was very pleased with what I saw; he was a browned skinned black guy standing about 6'3, definitely a step up from the bartender. He had a very smooth voice, reminding of the guy from the All State commercials, or at least he was pretending to. He sat in the bar stool right on the left of me. Even though the music was loud, we indulged in small talk for what seemed like forever. We went on to talk about my work and my break up with Lance. He seemed very compassionate and looked me in the eyes as I poured out my feelings. The whole time we talked, he held my hand and rubbed them with his thumbs. I've been in my relationship so long that I've forgotten what it's like to be flattered.

After a while, he offered to walk me back to my car. At this point I had at least five or six drinks. Feeling so tipsy I accepted his offer and allowed him to walk me to my car. In the parking lot he grabbed me by my waist from behind and kissed me softly on the back of my neck. Feeling so vulnerable I didn't have the strength or the will to fight him off. It felt so damn good to get this type of attention. I was immediately turned on by his quick attraction to me. He wasn't shy at all. I haven't gotten this attention in so long from Lance that it felt so good that I didn't want it to end. I grabbed him by the back of the head and gave him a deeply passionate kiss. I wanted him to know that I was feeling the same way, or even more. Being tipsy was definitely helpful in my forwardness. He asked if he could come back to my place, I told him NO and that I didn't even know his name. He playfully told me he'll tell me his name if I allowed him to come to my place. At this point I was so into him that I didn't want to ruin this moment with so many questions. He said that he'll trail me home to make sure I made it safely. Since I did have a bit much to drink, I didn't mind at all. I would admit that he was a smooth talker, and every bit of game that he was trying to spit at me was working. I knew that I normally don't get down like that with just a random person but I couldn't resist him.

I got in my car and waited for him to drive around to meet me so he could trail me home. I couldn't believe I was doing this but part of me just didn't want to be lonely. Normally, I would have been extremely nervous but the alcohol numbed my senses. I felt like I was watching myself outside of myself. I was having an outer body experience. I was telling myself no, but I was telling myself to go ahead at the same time. When he drove around to meet me, I wanted to just drive off quickly and leave him, but my damned heart needed this. My heart needed to feel secure and wanted. I was like a drug addict, I just had to have it. And that "it" was just some attention and affection. The whole way to my condo, I kept checking my review mirror to check to see if someone was trailing behind him. I had begun to get a little paranoid. I guess my buzz was coming down. What if Lance was out watching me the whole time? What if he actually set this whole thing up? In a way I was looking for the cameras and Joey Greco from Cheaters, even though technically I wasn't cheating. Whenever we would stop at a red light I would look in the review mirror trying to see if he looked the same way he did in the club. From what I could see, he did look a little bit older than I thought, which really didn't matter at all. The love of my life just broke my heart and this was God's way of making it okay. Or, at least I hoped it was. I deserved to be happy after being so good to Lance. I found every excuse in my own mind to make what I was doing okay.

When we got to the parking garage of my condo, he ran to open my car door for me. He was everything that I needed at this time, and damn he was so sexy. He grabbed my left hand and led me out of my car and closed the door for me. He was doing everything that Lance once did plus a bit more. When we got into my condo, we were all over each other, immediately. We were kissing and taking each other's shirts off. In the heat of the moment, I asked him if he wanted something to drink. He said "yes" and told me whatever I got is fine. The only thing I could think of was a bottle of expensive wine that Lance and I had bought in Venice, Italy for our first year anniversary together. Since Lance has voluntarily walked out of my life, I wanted to start at that moment of getting rid of everything that we shared together. We kept the wine in a small safe under our bed. I lead him to my room and told him to take his shoes off and get comfortable while I reached under the bed to open the safe. I ran to the kitchen and got wine glasses and when I got back to the room he had gotten completely naked. I poured the wine and downed my first glass quickly. I knew that it was going down tonight, so I wanted to get lit quickly.

I asked him if he had condoms and he then grabbed his pants off the floor and reached in to the pockets and pulled out a condom wrapped in a red metallic looking wrapper. I was a bit intrigued by the futuristic look of this condom wrapper. He sat the condom on my nightstand right next to the bed. I poured myself yet another glass of wine and took my time drinking it. In the midst of this time we were kissing and licking every part of each other. He had forced me on my back, held both my ankles up with one hand and proceeded to run his wet warm tongue from my back to my inner thigh. I was so intoxicated by then that I felt as if I was blacking in and out of ecstasy. There was nothing that was bringing me down. He entered me, with a smooth warm familiar force that I fell in love with instantly. All I could remember was that I was feeling good; better than I felt in a very long time. About twenty minutes had passed, and I came without him even touching me. He held my body so tight and came himself. The warmth of his breathe warmed my soul as he deeply exhaled. He held me tighter and kissed me like I he was going to die tomorrow. Feeling so high I didn't bother to get up and get a towel to clean up the sweat. I just didn't care. My heart had just been released from the Prison of Love and it wasn't turning back. I didn't want to leave this moment of ecstasy alone. I rolled over on my side to feel him cuddle up right behind me, reminding me of what Lance use to do. He wrapped his arms around me tightly, and I was out.

ALAN IV:

The next morning, I woke up facing the window. The sun reigned through the blinds onto my face and the still quietness of nothingness ringed at a high pitch in my ears. I quickly found myself in the middle of an episode of De Ja Vu. I looked around to see no sign of him. I then realized that he never told me his name. I laughed to myself on how ashamed I should have felt, but didn't. I know his presence wasn't an hallucination because I can smell his cologne in my sheets and plus there was the empty bottle of wine and two half filled wine glasses. I immediately was feeling my hangover so I grabbed both glasses and down the rest of the wine. I was once told the best way to get rid of a hangover is to drink more of what you were drinking and let it wear off during the day. Besides, this was some very expensive wine that I didn't want to waste.

I couldn't believe what I had done last night and I had begun to feel guilty. Even though Lance had left me, I still felt like I owed him me. He should have been the one in my bed last night. I began to cry once again and quickly snapped out of it. I was a great catch and any one would love to be with me. I'm cute, smart, independent and passionate, that's a lot for one person to offer. To be honest, I feel bad for Lance because he'll never find true happiness. Karma will hurt him bad or kill him at least. He'd have to go the ends of the world to begin to get close to the love and respect I had for him.

Since I didn't have any work scheduled for the next few days, I just sat at home and continued to feel sorry for myself. I didn't clean, shave or shower. I barely had the energy to cook or eat. I ordered pizza every day and each time I ate I just went back to bed. I was falling into a deep depression, quickly. I called Lance and Amanda' phones repeatedly and left messages.

Meanwhile, Tony would call me just about every two hours just to make sure I was alive. I greatly appreciated Tony for checking on me, he's the only reason why I haven't killed myself yet. I'm afraid that he'd call and I wouldn't answer, then he'll come over to my condo and find me dead. I didn't want to do that to Tony. He decided that I've wasted away long enough so he invited himself over.

Having Tony there just made me feel like I wasn't going through this horrible phase in my life alone. I loved how he'd do silly things just to make me smile and laugh. He came over with a huge birthday cake and balloons. He walked in singing the "Happy Birthday" song. I laughed hysterically because it wasn't even my birthday and it's just so random.

Later that night, I told Tony about my little episode with the guy from the club last night. He laughed and gagged at every detail. I told him how bad I felt for not knowing the guy's name, so Tony decided his name would be "Boy X". The "X" is just meaning he was anonymous or just simply unknown. Tony was proud of me for allowing myself to let loose, a little. He said he had someone that he wanted to hook me up with but I honestly wasn't in the mood for a new relationship. I'd rather lick my wombs for now and just focus on getting back to myself first. Besides, anybody Tony is trying to hook me up with is probably somebody he has already slept with. I know my friend means well, but no, I'm good.

ALAN V:

The next day when I woke up I felt strange. I felt like I may be coming down with a cold or something. My head felt heavily, my stomach was upset, and my body felt weak. I had a shoot scheduled that day and I needed to make sure my energy was on point. This photo shoot was for VIBE Magazine for the Atlanta based national recording boy group "Last Horizon". I was secretly a fan of this group. All of them were major sexy and I heard one of them just might be bi-sexual. Tony says he had seen the lead singer of the group Juan out at the gay clubs a while back. Tony also says he knows Juan ex-boyfriend David, but Tony swears he knows everybody and everything. All of that could be lies and fairytales. Leave it to Tony; everybody on TV and radio are all gay. It's not a huge secret that the music industry is filled with gay and bi-sexuals.

I told Tony about the shoot today and he was ecstatic. Since Tony was more excited than I was to be shooting "Last Horizon", I invited him along for the shoot. Having Tony there to assist me for the day actually worked out well. He wasn't loud and over barring like I thought he would be. He was extremely professional, even though I seen him trying to make small talk with the lead singer Juan. He did manage to ask Juan if he knew a David. Juan looked at Tony like he was going to burn a hole through his chest and said, "Yes, I do". He kept it short, cute and to the point. The group's manager Teresa was watching them like a hawk though. I can tell that she's controlling and treats them like puppies. I heard one of them even ask her if he could go use the restroom. Every time we asked the guys simple questions like, "when is the next song coming out", their manager would butt in and answer all the questions. Though they seemed like cool guys, I can tell that their manager had a tight leash around their necks. They didn't seem like the same suave guys that I've seen in the music videos. They seemed extremely meek and unpresent. I can tell there was a bit of tension in the group when it came to Juan. He really didn't seem to fit in with the rest of the guys. He didn't talk much with them or even the manager which left him open for questioning by Tony. Tony swears he's Oprah's son, with all the questions he's asking Juan. He's asking Juan questions like; "How do you plan to use your voice to help your community". Tony was trying to be funny with this question, because he was meaning the "gay community". Tony could be so messy at times but it allowed me to laugh a little.

Throughout the shoot I began to feel even worse. At the end of the shoot, Tony came back to my house to stay the night with me. I thought maybe I was feeling sick because of my break up with Lance. I guess this is what being "lovesick" was about. I took all the anti-biotic and fever reducers I had in my cabinet. Tony made me some soup but I threw it up. I told him I might be just coming down with a cold or the flu that's been going around. Even though I haven't heard of a flu going around that year, I figured there was always a new type of flu going around, so it was appropriate to think that.

ALAN VI:

The next day I was dead sick. I woke up and my body felt like a furnace. I was able to crawl out of bed and make it to the kitchen to get something to eat. Everything I ate seemed to have made me sicker. I ended up calling all my clients and canceled all my shoots for that week. I knew what ever this was wasn't going to go over night.

I went online that day and "Goggled" the symptoms that I was having and everything came back as the flu. At that time I didn't think it could be anything other than that. For a split second, I thought that it could be HIV, but that couldn't be so. I remember seeing "Boy X" with a condom in a red metallic wrapper. The more I sat and thought about that night, the more I began to get nervous. Though I remember seeing the condom, I can't remember him using it. Though I doubted that I being HIV positive was the case, I didn't want to ignore the worst case scenario.

After about three days I began to feel a bit better. I felt like I would feel 100 percent in just days, but that wasn't the case.

My throat began to hurt me so bad, to the point where I didn't want to talk, eat or even drink anything. I checked my throat in the mirror to find that my tonsils were swollen and discolored. They were very dark and the size of golf balls. Usually, I don't believe people when they say that their tonsils were as big as golf balls, but they were. I knew then that these symptoms were far more than what I was thinking they were. I was way too scared to go to the hospital, because I was afraid of what the truth may be. Whenever Tony or anyone else would call me I would pretend that I was feeling better. I would clear my throat before I answered the phone to make it seem as if I was up and about. I was really sick and not getting any better. I didn't want them to worry about me. Plus at this point I needed to deal with whatever this was, alone. Having more people to explain things to at this moment, was more than over whelming.

The next day when I woke up and went to the bathroom, I barely recognized myself in the mirror. There were dark circles around my eyes and my skin had begun to look pale. I looked dead to me, almost like one of those zombies in the movies. I knew whatever this was, was killing me. I decided then to go to the hospital. I shaved, took a shower and put on some clean clothes and headed to the hospital. The thought of me going to the hospital, made me feel good in the inside. I knew then that help was on the way. I began to not care what the outcome was going to be, I just wanted to feel better.

When I got to the emergency room I waited for about an hour before I was seen by a nurse. I was called to the back and the nurse began to check my vitals. The nurse asked me, what was the reason for my visit on that day. I told her that my tonsils looked swollen and I've been feeling feverish. She told me that there was indeed a "new flu" going around. Like I thought there is always a "new flu" going around. Though I joke about it, I hope this "new flu" is curable. She asked me several personal questions like; "when was the last time I had sex" and "do I practice safe sex." Of course I lied to her and said that I practice safe sex all the time, even though the last time I remember having unprotected sex was with Lance. Lance and I stopped using condoms about two years ago.

After the nurse was done she called in the doctor. The doctor introduced himself as Dr. Downie. He took a look at his notes that the nurse had gave him and asked me to open my mouth wide. I can tell by the expression on his face this was serious. He looked again at his notes and told me that I was running a fever of 102 degrees. He told me that he wanted to take some blood and send it in to the lab. He asked me if I practiced safe sex and I told him that I did. I can tell that he probably didn't believe me. I felt horrible for lying but I was so ashamed of myself. He told me that he will write me a prescription that will reduce the fever and the swelling of my tonsils. He even suggested that I get my tonsils removed. He told me that he will send the nurses into the room to do the blood work soon.

After about 20 minutes the nurse comes in the room with a small stack of papers, a needle, a thick rubber band and clear plastic tube. She explained to me that the paperwork was for me to sign giving permission to conduct an HIV/AIDS examination, and also a confidentiality agreement. I knew then that the doctor was probably thinking that this sickness maybe the worst thing that I could expect. I signed the documents and set back in the chair. The nurse asked me to stick out my right arm and to make a fist. She wrapped the rubber band around my arm and gave my vein a couple of taps before inserting the needle. She inserted the needle so hard that I felt the prick in my neck. I hated seeing blood so I had to look in the opposite direction as the blood poured into the clear plastic tube. After she drew my blood the nurse told me that it would take a week to get the results back and that they will call me once they were in.

I left the hospital feeling so empty, confused and hopeless. I couldn't believe this was happening to me. Just a couple of weeks ago, I was in what I thought was love, and healthy. Now I have no love and I'm sick, possibly. I went to a pharmacy and picked up my prescription and took them immediately. I went home right away to lie down because I began to feel very weak again.

ALAN VII:

The next day I woke up and felt so much better. Whichever medications the doctor had given me were working. I felt good enough to at least keep my regularly scheduled appointment for that day. Besides I haven't been working for a while and my bills were not going to pay themselves. I needed to get back to making some money. Thankfully, I made enough money to still afford where I was living without Lance. Plus, I've been able to save lot of money by splitting the rent with him all these years. I had planned to work on taking his name off the lease soon. Removing him from the lease would probably help me get over him.

While I was working, Tony called and said that he had something he wanted to show me. He seemed to be super excited to show me whatever it was. Knowing Tony, it's probably nothing important. We planned for him to come over that night after we both got off work.

Seeing Tony that night made me feel even better. We laughed as usual at his crazy antics. I asked him what was it that he had to show me, and he got really excited. He told me I was going to gag when I see it. He thumbs through his phone and then hands it to me. When I look at the phone I just see a picture of a black BMW truck. Then I noticed it's actually Lance's truck. I asked Tony where he took this picture at. He told me to swipe to the next picture. When I swiped to the next picture it was the same picture of the truck with the windshield busted out. I gasped for air, quickly stood up and asked Tony if he did this. My mouth opened in shock and I couldn't close it. I was immediately pissed at Tony. Tony says that he did it because he had no right to leave me like he did. Though I understood Tony for being a friend, I just wasn't going to make an excuse for him to bust Lance's windows out. He told me that he seen Lance at the grocery store but Lance didn't see him. He said when he got outside he seen Lance's truck and picked up a stone from the stores landscaping and smashed his window out. I couldn't believe this. I knew Tony was crazy but I didn't think he was this crazy. I'm sure Lance probably believes that I did this, or at least had something to do with it. Lance don't have any enemies, that I know of. I will be the only suspect. This just made things worse for me. I just wanted to simply move on with my life. Though I didn't express it, I was really disappointed with Tony.

A few days later while I was working, I received two missed calls from a private number. Immediately I was thinking that it was Lance. Maybe he has a new number and he wants to discuss what happened to his car. I begin to feel extremely nervous, I was never in trouble with the law but this could land me in jail. The worst thing of it all, is that I had nothing to do with it. Later that night when I got home I received another call from the private number so I answered. As soon as I said, "Hello", the person on the other end said, "Hey Bitch! That got me locked up for vandalism!" Right away I knew it was Tony and he was in jail. He says that Lance was able to identify him from the surveillance video from the grocery store's parking lot. So now I'm thinking that Lance believes that I put Tony up to that.

He says he may be facing some jail time, a fine and community service. He didn't seem to be too worried about being in jail. He actually sounded like he was having a good time. However, I know how Tony masks his true feelings about things that dramatically affects him. Tony told me one night while we both were drunk that he was raped and beaten by his stepfather. He said that he told his mom but his mom didn't believe him and sent him to live with his grandmother in Chicago. He says that his mom accused him of trying to ruin her already abusive relationship with his stepfather. Then after years of being raised by his grandmother while he was in high school he found her robbed, and murdered in her living room. She actually left a lot of money to Tony. He decided to drop out of school and moved back to Atlanta. He blames his stepfather for making him gay. Tony's been through so much in his life and being his friend hasn't been the easiest, but I wouldn't dare turn my back on him.

Tony and I have so much in common. Even though I wasn't molested growing up, I definitely know what it's like to be disowned by my parents. I came out to my parents after my first year in college. I only came out because I felt like I couldn't live the life I was living anymore. My mom and dad both told me I was no longer allowed in their home. I haven't been back to their home since which, was about nine years ago. I'm so hurt with just the fact that my parents have not tried to reach out to me at all. I tried to call them thousands of times over the years but they never answer. The last time I've seen my parents was about five years ago when I decided to surprise them at church on Mother's Day. My mom and my father both caused a huge scene in church by standing up and asking the church to pray for their "gay son, who has done the ultimate sin of sleeping with other men." I will never forget those words flowing from my dad's mouth and seeing my mom stand by his side and agree with all he said. I was so embarrassed and hurt that I vowed to never return to that church. I grew up in a very stable household. My mom was a nurse and my dad was a local Politician. I have two younger twin sisters that I rarely speak to. When I do talk to them I feel like I'm talking to total strangers. I can tell they are influenced by my mom and dad. We all grew up a very close family. We were the picture perfect family that was heavily into church. I played sports in high school and was even prom king. While I was in high school I had several girlfriends, but I never took them serious. I was only doing it, because I thought it was the "cool" thing to do. I often blamed myself for destroying my family. If I could just make myself interested in women I wouldn't have been so vulnerable to begin with. Me not having my family around made me extremely weak and dependent on other people in the world for love. When I met Lance he was everything that I was missing in my family. He filled every void and now that he's out of my life, I'm lost again.

ALAN VIII:

A few days later I received a call from the hospital telling me that I needed to come in as soon as possible. Even though the medication that I was prescribed was helping me feel better, I still didn't feel 100 percent. I was so nervous the whole ride to the hospital. I turned the music off completely. I just wanted to ride in silence so I could think clearly. When I arrived at the hospital I walked through the automatic sliding doors and felt the coldest sensation ever. I understood that the hospital is normally kept cool but this pure cold feeling of fear pulsated from the core of my bones. The same nurse that was there the week before seen me as I walked in and told me to come on back. She sat me in a private room off to itself and told me that she would be right back. The whole time she was gone my heart pounded so hard that I could feel it in my throat.

When the nurse came back in the room, she told right away that my test came back positive for HIV. She looked as devastated as I felt. I can tell that it was hard for her to deliver this news to me but she had to do her job....

After being diagnosed as being HIV positive of course my entire life changed. I felt like my walk and talk had changed, completely. I had become very bitter towards people. My patience for little things like; red lights and waiting in lines was no more. I felt like since I was going to die I was going to go out with a bang. I started to plan a bucket list of things to do before I die. Even though there are people living healthy lives with HIV, I felt like I wasn't going to be as lucky.

I was so embarrassed of my outcome I couldn't find the confidence to tell anyone, not even Tony. This news was so heavy that I couldn't really focus on my recent break up with Lance. I was actually glad that we were not speaking at all. He would have probably disowned me if he found out. His touch would definitely make me feel a bit better about life. I was really missing him. My emotions were up and down. I got a glimpse of what bipolar could be like. One minute I was optimistic, the next I hated life.

ALAN IX:

The more I set alone with my thoughts the more I allowed them to consume me. I wanted to find this guy that did this to me. I had to confront him about this. I wasn't sure what I would say to him but I knew I had to.

 I decided to go to Tricks every night to see if he would be there. After about a week and a half, I walked in and there he was at the bar talking to someone else. I stormed up to him and told him that I needed to speak to him. He looked at me as if he had never seen me before and told me to get the fuck out of his face. Though I came up to him really demanding, I wasn't prepared for him to tell me to get the fuck out of his face. I didn't care if I was going to cause a scene, because I was burning with revenge on the inside. This dude gave me a death sentence and I wanted make sure he paid for what he did to me. Feeling ignored I got in between him and the guy that he was talking with and said, "You gave me HIV". As soon as I said that he punched me so hard in the face that I fell to the floor. The other people in the nightclub started to gather around when security grabbed me up by my collar and drug me out the club. They told me to leave now or they were calling the police. I was trying to tell them that I didn't do anything and it was him that assaulted me.

Moments later another security guard was escorting Boy X out as he rubbed his hand. He looked dead at me and yelled, "Stay the fuck away from me, faggot." I told him that he's going to regret what he did to me. I walked back to my car feeling extremely weak but burning with anger. When I got in the car I looked at myself in the review mirror and noticed that the side of my face had a knot on it. This made me even more furious. Too bad Tony was still in jail or else I would have brought him back up to the nightclub to whip his ass. Before I left the parking lot, I could see him go back into the night club with the security guards. They were all looking back at my car as if they were waiting for me to leave.

I was so mad that I didn't feel like going home, so I just drove. The more I drove the angrier I got. I had made it up in my mind that Boy X had to die and I had to kill him. I was so convinced that this was the right thing to do. Being so angry I had no rational control over my emotions. I drove 20 minutes away to College Park. There was a part of College Park that was extremely dangerous at night. Tony told me years ago that he bought a gun from over here from a "Trap House". A "Trap House" is a place where lots of illegal exchanges take place like; drugs, stolen property, etc. Usually, I would have been scared as hell to come on this side of town alone, but I was in so much rage, it cancelled out my fear of this area. I knew that I should be able to find someone who I could buy a gun from around there. I've seen about five guys standing on a corner and I stopped the car and rolled down my windows. They all looked at me and put their hands on their waist like they're reaching for guns. They didn't know who I was and wanted to be prepared just in case I tried anything foolish with them. I asked them if they knew where I could buy a gun from, "Who in the hell are you?", "This dude is probably a cop", a couple of the guys were saying. "No no, I'm no cop", I said firmly. I was trying to sound hard using a deep urban accent. "What the fuck is wrong with your face", one of the guys asked laughing. "Somebody don' knocked his ass the fuck out", another guy added. "Yea, Cuz. What kind of gun you looking for", the tallest one asked. I told him I was just looking for any gun that's small and easy to shoot. He told me to follow them down the street to his uncle's house. He pointed to a house which was only about 300 feet away. He began to walk towards the house as I slowly trailed behind him.

The whole area around the house was completely dark. There were no street lights or even a porch light. Though I was still infuriated, this setting made me a bit uneasy. I wasn't sure if they were going to rob or try to kill me. The tall guy knocked on my window, told me to get out and follow him in the house. When I got into the house I was welcomed by the loudest aroma of marijuana that I've ever experienced. He told me to follow him down stairs to the basement. When we got down to the basement which was only lit with a small lamp he told me to wait there. He went inside this thick black door and I can hear other people in that room greeting him. He closed the door for a about a half of a minute. I figured he was telling his uncle or whoever, that I was there to buy a gun. He opened the door, stuck his head through and signaled for me to come in. When I got in the room there were three other guys there all with big blunts in their hands. I was trying to act as hard and straight as possible. I didn't want them to think for a second that I was some random sissy. One of the guys asked me right away, what kind of gun I was looking for. I told him that I needed something small and quiet. He told me he didn't want to know what I was going to do with it. He asked me how much I have to spend. I knew I had two one hundred dollar bills in my pocket so I pulled it out. I told him that was all I had. He said that he got a Nina, silencer and a loaded clip that he will sell to me for the two hundred. He could have been ripping me off but I didn't care. I handed over the money with no questions asked. He asked me if I knew how to use it and I told him no. He gave me a quick tutorial on how to load the clip into the gun and how to attach the silencer. Assembling this gun reminded me of assembling my cameras for work. Just a couple parts to snap together and I'm ready to shoot, literally.

ALAN X:

When I got back in my car I was still feeling like I wanted to kill. I couldn't believe he punched me in the face. When I looked myself in the review mirror I got mad all over again. The knot that I seen earlier grew even more. One side of my face was swollen. The more I thought about it the faster I drove. I was going to head back over to Tricks, to see if he had left yet. I don't remember what kind of car he had, so I had to wait across the street until the club lets out. I parked my car across the street and eyed the entrance of the night club. I sat there in silence. I didn't want to hear anything but my thoughts. Every thought I had was about me killing this dude. He's gotten away with murder and I was going to make him pay for it.

After waiting across the street for about 45 minutes, groups of people were leaving out of the night club and congregating in the parking lot. I spotted him walking to his car, talking to the same guy that he was talking to when I confronted him. He got in his car and rode around the parking lot to where the other guy parked. When the other guy gets in his car they both leave with Boy X trailing behind him. This seemed like the same scenario I had with him. I didn't have a plan, I just followed behind him. I tried to stay a couple of cars behind so that I wasn't so obvious.

We finally end up in Marietta, at an apartment complex that's about five minutes away from my condo. Though it's dark outside the apartment complex's parking area is lit very well with street lights. I decided to park in an area that wasn't lit at all which was only about 100 feet away. They parked next to each other, with Boy X parked on the right. I got out of my car and walked over to Boy X's car. By the time I approached his car, he had just opened the car door and was fixing to get out. The other guy was still sitting in his car looking like he was looking down at his cell phone. When Boy X stood up from getting out of the car I yelled, "So who's the faggot?" He turned around towards me quickly as if he was startled. I shot two times. I shot him once in the face and in the chest. He didn't have any time to respond. After I seen him fall to the ground my adrenaline rushed through my veins so fast that I could taste it. The other guy got out of his car and began to scream. I walked over to his driver side and shot him three times. I felt like I was outside of my body and I had no control. I felt like a robot and all I could see was red. I quickly ran back to my car and drove away fast.

When I got back into my car I was breathing hard. I couldn't believe what I had just done. I just killed two people. I am that guy that I've watched on those shows where people snap. Something inside of them triggers them to do horrible things to people. I've always been a level headed individual, I couldn't believe I allowed this to happen to me. I began to panic and feel extremely paranoid. I didn't drive directly to my condo, because I was afraid that someone may have seen me and followed me. Suddenly I seen three police cars zoom past me going toward the scene with their sirens on. I knew then that I had to find away to hide the gun.

I rushed to my condo so I could get rid of the gun. I wasn't thinking clearly at all. When I got into my condo the only place I could think to put the gun was in the safe under my bed. I ran into my room and felt under my bed to pull out the safe. When I slid the safe from under the bed, I noticed that an opened red metallic condom wrapper slid out with it. There was also a used condom stuffed inside, tied in a knot with seaman in it. It looked as if, it could have accidently been kicked under the bed. I picked it up and looked at it closely. My panic and paranoia turned into immediate guilt, shame and shock. I was an emotional cocktail. I fell to the floor crying and weeping. I couldn't believe this whole time I thought he didn't use a condom that night. The proof was right under me and I didn't realize it. All I could think was that I just killed two innocent guys for no reason. I grabbed the gun and slowly put it to my head. I closed my eyes when all of sudden my phone rings. I slowly slid my phone from my pocket to see that it's Lance...

THE B O Y X

CHRONICLES

LANCE CALLOWAY

Birthday: October 14
Sign: Libra
Occupation: Model
Highest Education: Associates Degree in Communication
Personality Type: Motivated Dreamer, Indecisive

LANCE

I gave into my feelings and decided to call Alan. I was having trouble trying to wrap my mind around how my life was about to change and how he just wouldn't understand. After about four rings he answered the phone. He didn't seem to have much emotion at all. Or maybe he just had a lot on his mind. "Sorry to call you so late, you were really on my mind all day. I wanted to see how you were doing", I said feeling guilty. "Oh ok. I, I, I have... I'll call you back", he strangely stuttered as he hung up the phone. I could understand if he didn't really want to hear from me. I left him cold, with no warning at all. I felt bad for doing what I did. It was the only way I knew how to handle what I was going through. I loved Alan so much that I couldn't stand to tell him the truth. Feeling anxious I called him back. This time he didn't answer...

LANCE I

A few months ago I was offered a modeling gig in Venice, Italy for a new international magazine. By that time I had already told Alan that he should no longer be my assistant. It was only because I felt like we were spending way too much time together. I wanted to put some space between us, thinking that that would bring us closer. The space I allowed actually drove us further apart. Not seeing Alan so much was like the old saying "out of sight, out of mind". Whenever I was away, our relationship didn't seem to matter as much as it did when we were together all the time. I was able to make my own decisions without considering Alan, especially when I was out of the country.

While I was at the shoot for the magazine in Venice, I was invited to go to the magazine's launch party. The night of the launch party, I was presented with the opportunity to star in an Italian porn movie. I have never considered doing porn in my life. As a matter of fact I didn't have a lot of respect for porn stars. The amount of money I was offered to star in this movie was hard to pass by. I was thinking that I would use this money to save up to buy a house for Alan and I, somewhere in Los Angeles. I agreed to shoot the movie in which I would be the only bottom in a bareback orgy of six other guys. While I was ensured that everything was safe and clean I still was extremely hesitant. I haven't been a bottom in a very long time and I'm not sure how I should prepare myself for this movie. The shoot was to take place a day before I was to fly back to the U.S. and then home to Atlanta. I thought this allowed me time to recover from the shoot.

When I got back to Atlanta I was beyond exhausted. I wasn't in the mood for anything. I loved Alan, but for some reason I found it hard to build up the emotion to be affectionate toward him. I often felt bad for it but I also felt like it was partially his fault. Even though he did nothing wrong, it was his fault. He actually started to work out more and experimenting with his look a bit. I really appreciated him for "re-inventing" himself even though he was already perfect in my eyes. There was nothing wrong with him. It was all in me. I was ashamed of myself for not only cheating but the way I cheated was all too much. I just hoped and prayed that Alan or anyone he knew never saw that movie, especially his crazy friend Tony.

I never liked Tony. He has always been loud and too much to handle. He wasn't a good influence on Alan and I made it clear to him that I felt that way. Whenever he came around I noticed a change in Alan. I understood that he would act differently around a close friend but the way he acted around Tony was a major turn off. He would swear and begin to use all the "Gay Lingo", that just annoyed me. I.E; "What's the tea", "Shady Boots", "Gurt", "To the Gods"... When it was just Alan and I, he was always so quiet, kind and sweet. He was extra responsible unlike Tony, who does nothing with himself. He had already been to jail for theft and for fighting in a night club.

Just a couple of weeks ago I walked outside of the grocery store to find that my windows in my truck were bashed out. When I first saw my truck, the first person I thought of was Tony. I knew that this was probably retaliation for me walking out on Alan. I knew that Alan wasn't the type of person to do something like that. I called the police. When they came they asked me if I knew anyone who would have had a reason to do that to my car. I immediately told them Tony's name, without being 100 percent sure he did it. When the police department got the parking lot surveillance camera footage from the grocery store, I was able to witness and identify Tony bashing my windows out of my car. Seeing him throw a brick through my window made me furious. I wanted to find and beat him myself. On the flipside, seeing that brick through my window made me see how hurt Alan must have been when I left him. I didn't think I was capable of causing so much pain to someone else, but I did. I sat and watched my phone ring every time Alan called. I was so tempted to answer it but I just couldn't. I knew I was no longer who he thought I was. I was dirty. I was nasty. I was contaminated. I was HIV positive.

LANCE II

A lot has changed since I've walked out on Alan. I had now moved into a smaller apartment on Rowell Road, which was about 15 minutes away. Since I left Alan I haven't had a paying gig. The money that I had saved while I was with Alan was enough to live on for several months but I had to get back to work somehow. With my new condition, I honestly didn't have the confidence to apply for any modeling gigs. The work I would get would have to come from The Trusey Agency that I've already worked for. Trusey is one of the top modeling agencies in the Atlanta area. Its CEO Mark Trusey was once a very popular model back in the 1980's and through the 90's. Mark was more than a boss to me; he was a mentor and big brother. I met him years ago back in Los Angeles at a fashion show for Victoria Secrets. Back then he was working as a recruiter for Victoria Secrets, and actually approached me about modeling for him once he got his own agency started. Since I've always wanted to model and I knew his track record, I agreed to re-locate to Atlanta to work.

I called the agency twice a day to see if they had any gigs but nothing was coming in. I even got desperate enough to ask Mark if I could possibly work for the agency as a recruiter. Since I've worked with this agency for years now, Mark understood me wanting to at least work since nothing was coming up for me. Mark offered me a position as an office receptionist. Their previous office receptionist was a no call, no show for days so they decided to hire me. Even though I wasn't making the amount of money that I would if I worked in front of the camera, it felt good to make money again.

My first days of work were extremely busy. The Trusey Agency was having an open model call. I found it quite strange that we were doing open model calls BUT they couldn't find me any work. I was once they're top male model. My pictures are enlarged and hung all over the office walls along with some of the other models. Since the office was located in the middle of Downtown Atlanta which is easy to find, the open model call was busy with a line that wrapped out the front door and ended in front of a business that was three doors down. For the open calls it was my job to hand out applications and to take head shot photos of the aspiring models. Even though most of the models would bring their own head shots, it was important for Mark to know how they looked in person just in case their headshots were photo shopped.

After about three hours of the open call in walks a 6'1, muscularly lean white guy, wearing a black tank top, with tight lightly colored blue jeans showing his nicely sculptured legs and ass. Since I've worked in the modeling business I'm rarely impressed with the looks of another guy but damn, he was fine. Welcome to The Trusey Agency", I said as I handed him an application. "Thank you, aren't you Lance. Lance Calloway", he asked. "Oh. Yes. Yes I am", I said stuttering almost forgetting my own name. "It's nice to meet you Lance. I'm very familiar with your work", he said. Immediately my mind went to the porn I did in Italy. I hope he wasn't talking about that. Even Mark knew nothing of that, and if he ever found out, I'm sure he'd be disappointed in me. "Thanks so much. I appreciate that. So what's your name", I asked quickly turning the conversation back to him. "My name is Tyler. I just moved here from Vegas", he said. "Well welcome to Atlanta. Stand against the wall there", I said as I pointed to the wall to the left of the room. He turned around and walked over to the wall as my eyes immediately scanned his body from head to toe. He turned back to me and gave me a smile and a wink, as if he knew I was admiring his backside. "Okay. Good. Keep that smile", I said jokingly as I snap the picture. "Nice", I said as I looked at the picture on the digital display screen. "Can I see", he asked laughing. "Umm. Maybe later", I said jokingly. "So what's next", he asked. You're going to go down the hall and wait outside of the door. They'll call you in once they're ready for you", I said as I pointed to the door of the room where Mark was conducting his face-to-face quick interviews with the potential models. He walked down the hall as I got a chance to look at his nicely built body once again.

I sat back down behind my desk and about a minute later I could hear Mark, "Thanks for coming Stacey, see my receptionist Lance, he'll give you a brochure of all the classes we are offering. Hello and your name is..". "My name is Tyler", I heard him say from down the hall. Seconds later Stacey had made her way up to the front to me. "Can I get the brochure for the classes you offer?" she asked. "Yes you may", I replied as I reached for a brochure from the stack of brochures on my desk. "Hey, aren't some of these pictures of you"?, she surprisingly asked. "Yes they are of me", I said with a smile. "So can you tell me more about being a model, like how did you get started"?, she asked. Just I was about to answer her, Mark and Tyler walks to the front where my desk is situated. Mark grabbed a brochure from my desk and handed it to Tyler. Mark then walks Tyler to the door and shakes his hand before he walked out. I was immediately annoyed with Stacey, because I'd rather be talking to Tyler. I wanted to talk with him before he left. She was cock blocking with all the questions she was asking. After I finished giving her a quick spill of being a model, with the biggest smile she reached to shake my hand and said, "It's a pleasure meeting you". "Thanks, same here", I said. "Thanks for stopping by Stacey. I hope to see you at our classes", Mark says as she makes her way out the door.

"And another successful open call", Mark says to me. "Yes, absolutely", I said. "You know Lance, if you would like to make more money, you could come to teach some of the modeling classes", Mark said. "Absolutely. I could use the extra cash", I said. "Good, the classes start next week. I could use you to teach the male models how to walk a runway for urban clothing lines. You're more hip in that area than me", he said laughing. "Well thanks Marky Mark. I'll do my best", I said playfully. "Take these applications and file them for me. Once you're done you can go ahead and leave", he said as he handed me a stack of about two hundred applications. When he walked away I looked at the top of the stack to see Tyler's application there. I immediately took out my cell phone and snapped a picture of his application. I wanted to get his contact info from the application. After taking the picture I quickly filed the applications and left.

On the application he provided a cell number and email address. I did notice that he didn't write down an address though, I thought since he just moved here from Vegas he probably didn't remember his address at the time. I debated in my mind if I should use the information that Tyler provided on the application to contact him. I didn't want to seem like a stalker. Even though I was tempted I decided not to. I know that Mark gave him a brochure, so maybe he'll show up for a few classes at the agency.

LANCE III

When I arrived home that evening I was feeling weak. I took my medication and lay down to take a nap. I woke up to my phone ringing and was Amanda. "Lance, did you hear"?! she said frantically. "Hear about what?", I asked as I trying to wake myself up. "About Alan. He's missing. I just saw it on the news", she said sounding out of breath. "Are you serious? That can't be real. I just spoke to... Let me call you back", I said as I quickly hung up the phone. I grabbed the remote to the TV set and turned it on. I quickly shuffled through the channels to the news. It was on commercial. I impatiently turned to the next news station and it was also on commercial. I picked my phone up and called Amanda back. As soon as she answered I asked, "what channel did you see that on"? "Channel 5, I just seen it", she said as I hung up the phone not even saying bye. I turned to Channel 5 and there is was. "Two Men Killed and one missing in Atlanta". My mouth dropped. The reporter says that Alan's car was identified leaving the scene where two guys were shot and killed. I frantically tried to call Alan hoping that he'd answer but he didn't. I knew something wasn't right.

I kept the TV tuned into the news, I was hoping to find out more of what was going on with Alan. Amanda called me back, "I'm on my way to your place", she said as soon as I answered the phone.

About twenty minutes later, Amanda was knocking at my door. "Are you okay?" she asked as I opened the door. She gave me a hug and we went into the living room to watch the news. "Have you spoken to Alan since we left the condo?" she asked. I paused, tears began to stream from my eyes. "I had the urge to call Alan the other night, so I did. When he answered he didn't sound like himself. I could tell he wasn't well. He told me he'd call me back, but he never did. I tried to call him back, but he never answered. I don't think Alan would kill anyone. He's not that type of person at all... or.... Maybe I turned him into that type of person", I said crying. Amanda grabbed me tightly as she also began to cry. For the rest of the night, we just set up watching the news hoping they had more to say about Alan's situation. We eventually fell asleep with the TV on. When I woke up Amanda was getting ready to go home. She'd since met and moved in with a guy named Marcel that lived in Dunwoody, which was only about 20 minutes away. She gave me a hug and a kiss on the forehead before she headed out of the door.

I turned to all the news stations in Atlanta just to see if they had found out anymore about Alan. Nothing was being said but the weather forecast which predicted rain all day. A gloomy day to go along with my gloomy life.

LANCE IV

    Eventually, I had to get up and get ready for work. When I arrived at the office there were police officers there. They were talking with Mark. Mark looked sad as if he wanted to cry. I felt like so many bad things were happening and I just didn't want to be involved with any more bad news. After the police left, Mark came to my desk and said, "Well, now I know why my old receptionist was a no call, no show. He was killed the other night. I can't believe this. Senseless…", he said shaking his head. "I'm sorry to hear that Mark. Well do you remember my boyfriend, Alan. Well I found out he's missing", I said sadly. Mark looked at me hard, he gave me a mean stare as if he was thinking hard about something. "What's Alan's last name", he asked. "Kline", I replied. "Oooh noooo… They're looking for him. They're saying he killed Randy. Oh Lance, I'm so so sorry. If you would like to take the day off, I would definitely understand", he said concerned. "I'll be okay, I think. I need something to do to keep my mind off of Alan. I just hope he's okay. I don't know what would have drove him to do such a thing".

This rainy day seemed to drag by slowly as I set at my desk looking at the large flat screen television in the reception area. I kept the news on all day. While Mark conducted his classes down the hall my eyes were glued to the TV. I only had to check in all the students, and take their payments for that day's classes.

As the day was ending, Mark's last class for that day had only about 10 minutes before it started when Tyler walked in. I honestly wasn't in the mood to entertain my little crush I had. I still was very nice to him when he walked. "Hello, Mr. Calloway. How's your day going?" Tyler asked. "I'm doing okay. Seen better days. Here just sign your name on the sign in list", I said faking a smile. As he bent down to sign the list on my desk my eyes caught a glimpse of the TV. "Alan Kline, found dead in his condo an hour ago" rolled across the screen of the news. I gasped for air as Tyler looked up at me with the side eye. "Oh my God. MARK", I screamed. I would have usually been a bit embarrassed for how I screamed but this was painful. "Oh no, wha.. wha.. What's wrong?", Tyler asked grabbing my shoulders. I just dropped my head on my desk and cried uncontrollably. Mark came running from down the hall. "What's going on Lance", he said as he came behind my desk to hug me. After about a minute I took a deep breath and told him they just found Alan dead. "Oh I'm so sorry to hear that Lance. Is there anything you would like me to do? You should go home for the day. How about you leave your car here and I take you home?", he asked concerned. "I think I'll be okay, I need some air. I'll be back...", I said still crying. I got up and walked outside just to breathe.

Without any thought, I stood in the rain gasping for air. The rain helped mask my tears, but couldn't make its' way to wash the filth from my heart. I felt horrible. I knew that this was somehow my fault. I grabbed my phone out of my pocket and called Amanda. I could barely get it out when she answered. She was able to make out what I was saying though. She cried hard on the phone and told me that she would have to call me back. When I hung up from Amanda, Tyler walked outside and put his arms around my shoulders. "I know you don't know me like that but I would like to be here for you", he said. I was having a bad moment and to be honest it felt good to hear him say that. I turned around to look at him with tears in my eyes, "Thank you. I'm going through a lot in my life right now. Please don't judge me. I just found out some really bad news and I've never experienced something like this in my life". "How about we go get a cup of tea from the café up the street?" he asked. "Wait. Aren't you here for your classes with Mark? I don't want to take you away from that", I said. "Oh, it's okay. I was actually only coming to meet with Mark, to tell him that I'm not going to be able to take his classes. Some things came up and I don't think I'll be able to afford it at this time", he said. "Oh wow... You're going through enough. You don't need my problems man", I said. "No, I insist. Let me get you a cup of tea", he said. Without another word I just nodded as we began to walk down the street toward the café. Tyler just seemed like an angel from heaven at that moment. Here he is going through his own issues but he's helping me through mine. I was blown away by his generosity.

When we got inside the café, he asked me what I wanted which was a green tea. He ordered us both the same drink. When our order was ready he grabbed both cups of tea and headed to a table by the window. He set down both cups and before I could even reach the table he had begun to pull out my chair. I was very puzzled but flattered by his actions. I have never been treated so kind by another guy. I'm usually the one who does all the cute nice stuff. This is exactly what I needed at this time but I swear it was all just too soon. I just found out Alan was found dead and here is this guy taking me out not even five minutes afterwards. "I'm so sorry to hear about your friend", he said. "Thank you. Sorry if I may seem a bit 'out of it', this is all new to me and... I'm trying to understand it all", I said looking out the window. When I turned to look back at Tyler, I caught a gulp of his beautiful light brown eyes. The sight was so unexpected, but pleasant that I was hypnotized for a few seconds. He just seemed so perfect. There was something angelic about him.

He grabbed my left hand with both his hands and began to gently massage my hand. I honestly didn't know for sure he was gay until now. "I would like to be here for you…" he started to say as my phone rang. I slid my phone from my pocket and it was Amanda. I answered the phone. "Are you okay? I'll stop by later tonight if you would like me to", she said. "Sure that'll be good. I'm going to try to see if I could reach his friend Tony, later tonight", I said. "Okay, I love you Lance", she said before hanging up the phone.

After the call ended, I slid my phone back in my pocket. "Do you have to go? If you have to go, please don't feel like you have to stay for me", Tyler said. "Oh no, it's fine. That's my friend Amanda. She wanted to make sure I was okay. She's stopping by my place later tonight", I said as I picked up my cup and began to sip. "Can I come to your place", he asked innocently. I almost spit my hot tea in his face. I couldn't believe how forward he was especially since he doesn't know me that well. "Sure, if you'd like", I said. "Only if you don't mind. Like I said I would like to be there for you", he said. For some reason, I got a little angry. I just wasn't accepting how generous he was being to me. "For me?! I don't need you here for me. Wait… You don't even know me Tyler. You've only just met me the other day. I could be the worst person you've ever met", I said feeling a bit agitated. "There's no way you can be like my Mom. That's the worst person I've ever met. There's something special about you. I want to be a friend to you", he said. "Okay. We can be friends", I said nodding. To be honest, if I wasn't going through so much at the time I would have been pursuing him with no problem. I felt like this was happening at the wrong time and too fast.

After drinking our tea we got up to leave the café. When we got outside, I made my way back toward The Trusey Agency building, so I could get in my car and head home. "Well, thanks for the tea, I will see you some other time", I said to Tyler. "Oh, so I'm not going to your place?" he asked. "Umm. No. I wasn't serious. Where's your car", I asked. "I don't have a car. I rode the bus over here", he said looking away. "Where do you live, I can take you home", I said. "Near Mid-Town", he said uncertainly. "Ok get in", I said. He walked over to the passenger side and got into the car.

As we began to drive off, I could tell he felt a bit nervous. I felt like he was hiding something. "So you just moved here from where again:, I asked. "From Las Vegas. I'm staying with a friend in Mid-Town", he said slowly. "Cool. How long have you known this friend", I asked. "Well honestly... I just met him on Craig's List before I moved here. He was looking for a roommate", he said. "Nice. So what makes you want to get into modeling", I asked. "I've been told by lots of people that I should try it. So I discovered The Trusey Agency", he said. For the next twenty minutes we discussed my modeling career and his big aspirations to become a model. As I drove along he told me to stop at a random "Waffle House" in Mid-Town. He said that he wanted to get a bite to eat from there and his place was only around the corner. I felt like he wasn't telling me the truth, but I just went a long with it. When he opened the door to get out of the car I asked him for his phone number. He said that his phone battery died earlier that day and he couldn't remember his new Atlanta number. I wasn't buying that though. He asked if he could get my number instead. I opened my glove compartment, took out a pen, ripped a piece of paper from an old envelop and wrote my number on it. I handed it to him, to see that he had the biggest smile on his face. "Wow, I just got a celebrities phone number", he said. "I'm no celebrity. Just a well known model. Thanks though. Have a nice day Tyler", I said as he closed the door. I began to drive away when I looked in my rearview mirror and saw that he was watching me drive away. There was something strange and unsettling about Tyler but damn I was really loving the attention.

LANCE V

When I got on the highway my thoughts went straight to Alan. I burst into a loud sobbing cry. I needed this time alone so I could get it out. I could only think of the good times we've had. I couldn't believe I was so mean and cruel to him and now he's gone forever. When I got home I ran to my bed to cry even more. I cried to the point where my head had began to hurt. I felt alone now. I loved no one like I loved Alan. About an hour of me lying in bed crying and thinking of Alan, I heard a knock at my door. I went to open the door and it was Amanda. She gave me a tight hug as she came in. We set in the living room and began to reminisce a bit about Alan. It was good to remember the good things. Having Amanda there felt really good, because she knew my relationship with Alan better than anyone else.

After about two hours of consoling each other, I decided with the help of Amanda to call Tony. Even though Tony and I didn't get along much, I knew we could put that to the side for now. I still had his number in my phone even though we never spoke. I wanted to know from Tony if there were any memorial services being planned for Alan. When he answered the phone I felt like he knew why I was calling. He seemed to have an attitude but still willing to hear from me. "Hey Tony, I just wanted to say I'm sorry for what happened to Alan", I said slowly. The whole time I'm on the phone with Tony, Amanda just set there consoling me. "Lance, I'm glad you called. I'm sorry this has happened to you also. Alan was extremely hurt by how you left him. I don't want to point the finger at you because you don't deserve to live with that guilt. Just know he really loved you", Tony said sadly. I've never heard Tony be so serious in my life. I never thought he could be. He always seemed loud and overly 'ghetto acting' to me. I expected him to want to curse me out. I asked him if he's heard anything from Alan's family, he told he was able to get in touch with one of his sisters. He said Alan's family is having him cremated with no memorial service. I couldn't believe that. I do know that Alan's family never dealt well with him being gay. I know he rarely spoke to them while we were together.

After hanging up with Tony I felt like crap. It hurt me to think that Alan's family didn't think he was important enough to at least have a memorial service. They were just going to burn him like he was trash. Trash that I loved, but also threw away like he meant nothing.

About 9 o'clock that night, Amanda left to go home. I received a called from a number that I didn't recognize, so I didn't answer. Curiously, I Googled the number on my phone and it came up as a Waffle House in Mid-Town. I knew then it had to have been Tyler. I couldn't understand why he was calling me from that Waffle House that I dropped him off at earlier. My phone rang again from the same number. I answered. "Hello Lance, I'm sorry to bother you so late", he said sadly. "Oh no, it's okay. How are you? Is everything okay", I asked. "Um... I need a place to stay for the night. I don't have anywhere to go", he said hesitantly. "I'm sorry to hear that. Are you asking if you could stay here for the night", I asked. "I would understand if you said no", he said. "Oh no, I'm not saying no. I'll be there to get you. Don't move", I said. "Thanks bro, I really appreciate this", he said. "No problem. I'll be there in a few", I said as I hung up the phone.

When I arrived to the Waffle House, I was a bit puzzled to see Tyler standing outside in the rain. He was wearing a hoody and holding two duffle bags. He looked like a scared puppy when I pulled up. He got in the car soaked with rain water, "Why didn't you just wait inside for me", I asked as soon as he got in the car. "I didn't want you to have to wait for me to come out", he said. I was still confused, there's no way I would have waited in the rain. I would admit I was impressed by his thoughtfulness, but he should've thought about not getting my car seats wet. "So... I'm not sure if you're up to answering any of my questions but... what happened to where you were staying?", I asked as if I was his parent. "I... Well, my roommate was unexpectedly evicted from his apartment today and since he had to leave I also had to leave", he said. "So where did he go? Don't you know other people here in Atlanta", I asked. I was actually feeling a bit pissed because I was feeling a bit used. Even though I really had no reason to, I just wasn't comfortable with the idea that I was his only source of contact. I had my own problems dealing with Alan's death and now this. "I don't know anyone else here. If this is a problem, I totally understand. You can just drop me off at the nearest train station", he said. There was a moment of silence that was ever so awkward. "I don't mean it like that. I don't have a problem with it. I'm glad you called me. I'm glad to help. I'm just going through a lot at this time in my life", I sad slowly. "I understand. I'm here for you", he said placing his left hand on top of my right hand which was resting on the armrest in between us. Feeling a bit awkward and just unprepared for the gesture, I slid my hand from under his hand and pretended to rub my eye. "There's something in my eye. It's been bothering me for a while now", I said. I was so lying and I'm sure he could tell. However, I really appreciated his kindness. I was definitely intrigued but afraid to react on my feelings. "Do you want me to blow it out", he asked. "Blow what out", I asked quickly. "Whatever it is that's in your eye", he said laughing. "No, I'm fine. So tomorrow... What's your plan for tomorrow" I asked seriously. "Well I'm planning to go to the bus station and head back home to Vegas", he said. "Mmm... Nice. That sucks you had no luck here in Atlanta", I said. "Yes, it does suck. That's typical for my life though. Nothing seems to work out the way I hope", he said sadly. From the tone in his voice, I could tell that he was really hurting but I couldn't think of anything I could do to help him and myself at that time.

When we arrived back to my building the rain had intensified. I parked the car and asked him to hand me my umbrella from under the passenger seat. He grabbed the umbrella, his two duffle bags and opened his door and got out with it. Immediately I was pissed. I was thinking he was going to use my umbrella for himself but no. He came to the driver side and opened the door for me, holding the umbrella over my head to I wouldn't get wet. I've never been so flattered in my life. He put his arms around my shoulders as I led the way to my apartment. Having his arms around me, I was able to feel how wet his clothes actually were.

When we got inside my apartment, I asked him if he wanted me to throw his wet clothes in my dryer. "Sure. Thanks. This is a nice place you have here", he said. "You're welcome and thanks. You can change your clothes in the bathroom", I said as I pointed down the small hall. He went into the bathroom to change as I turned on the TV. The TV was still turned to the news station I was watching earlier that day. I didn't want to hear anymore about the Alan's death. I was emotionally drained and still feeling really hurt. I turned to Comedy Central with hopes of watching something funny to help clear my mind. Moments later Tyler walked out of the bathroom and into the living room. He was only wearing a pair of red gym shorts that came up to his mid thigh. I was honestly immediately turned on by the view he was giving. His body was more ripped than mine. He definitely had a perfect model figure. "Dude, where's the rest of your clothes", I asked a bit annoyed. I was only pretending deep down, but I didn't want him to think he could just walk around my place half naked. "Oh, I'm sorry I wanted to ask if you minded if I took a shower", he said. "Oh. No I don't mind. Go ahead. There are extra bars of soap in the cabinet under the sink. There's a towel inside that little closet next to the bathroom door", I said as I pointed him back to the bathroom. "Thanks. Here are my wet clothes", he said handing them to me. I took his clothes and headed to my little laundry room next to the kitchen while he went to take a shower. Before I threw his clothes in the drier, I decided to check his pockets to make sure I didn't ruin anything that may have been left inside. I reached in the back pocket of his jeans and pulled out three wet business cards. One was a card from an escort service that had a name written on the back. Another one was from the Salvation Army. The last one was from The Trusey Agency, which had my number written on the back. I was saddened by this discovery. He was struggling to make it and apparently he's considered escorting to make money...

About ten minutes later he walked out of the bathroom with the same shorts on but this time he had a tight white V-neck t-shirt on. He walked into the living room and set on the couch next to me. "So can I ask you something", he asked me. "Sure, what is it", I said. "Who were you crying over earlier today", he asked. I took a deep breath. "I was crying because I found out my ex-lover was found dead. He committed suicide", I said slowly looking at the floor. "Wow, I'm so sorry to hear that. If you need someone to talk to I'm here... of course", he said. "Thanks Tyler. I appreciate your concern. So what time am I taking you to the bus station tomorrow", I asked changing the subject. "You can take me in the morning before you go in for work", he said softly. "Cool. I have to wake up around 7am so I can be at the office by 9am. It's now 11:45", I said looking at the clock on my living room wall. "Ok. That'll work for me", he said. "Your clothes should be done in a little while. You can sleep there on the couch. I'll bring you a blanket and pillow", I said as I got up from the couch heading to my room. I grabbed the throw blanket from the foot of my bed and a pillow from my bed to give to him. "Thanks, and goodnight", he said as I handed him the blanket and pillow. "Goodnight", I said as I walked back to my room. I immediately set my alarm clock that sat on a night stand next to my bed. I stripped down to everything but my tight black and red stripped underwear and got in my queen sized bed. I turned my light out, got under the covers and immediately began to cry. I was trying to stay as quiet as possible. I didn't think Tyler could hear me because the TV was still on. I cried hard baring my head into the pillows to hopefully mute my sobbing.

LANCE VI

The next morning I woke up to my alarm clock and in the arms of Tyler. He was holding me close from behind. Though I was under the covers he was on top of the covers just holding me. I didn't even feel him climb into bed with me. He set up and reached over me to turn off my alarm clock. "How long have you been in here", I asked. "I came in about an hour after you went to bed. You were crying in your sleep so I came to hold you", he said. I was speechless. I couldn't get mad him. It did feel good to wake up to him being there. "I'll go ahead and grab my things so you can take me to the bus station" he said. "Ok. I'm going to jump in the shower and prepare for work", I said. When he walked out of the room, I grabbed my cell phone that was sitting on my night stand. I turned on my phone to see that Mark had texted me hours ago, saying that he was giving me the day off. He wanted to give me time to deal with Alan's death.

I lay back in my bed looking at the ceiling thinking about all that was going on. I could hear Tyler walking through my apartment gathering his things to go. I jumped up quickly and walked into the living room to see Tyler putting on his now dry pants. I walked past him and grabbed both of his duffle bags and started to walk back to my room with them. "What are you doing", he asked quickly as he followed me into my room. I threw the bigger of the two bags on my bed and unzipped it. I began to take everything out. "You're going to stay here... Just for a little while until you get on your feet" I said smiling. "Whoa... Lance, I, I, don't know what to", he said as I cut him off. "Say? Say, nothing. Not even thank you. I'm going to help you, like you're going to help me. We're going to help each other", I said as I turned to look at him. At that moment our hearts aligned. Our eyes were locked on each other. Our souls had just been introduced. He walked toward me and gave me a hard deep passionate kiss. I can tell that he has wanted to do that for a long time. He pushed his duffle bag to the floor and pushed me back on the bed.

On my back I felt open, he could have me anyway he wanted. He gently bit on the right side of my neck as I closed my eyes to endure every bit of this ecstasy. My legs wrapped around his body tightly as he began to slide down my underwear. When I opened my eyes I saw Alan standing in the door of my room behind Tyler. I quickly jumped up and pushed Tyler off me as the image of Alan quickly faded away. "I'm sorry. I'm sorry. I didn't mean to move so quickly", Tyler said. "Oh no. No, it's not you. I think we should go slow. Very slow. There's a lot you should know about me", I said still looking at my room door. I was frightened and dazed at the image of Alan. I thought my mind was playing tricks on me. "Like what? I'm here to help you", he said as he began to sit up and noticed that I was staring at my room door. "Are you okay? You look like you seen a ghost", he said laughing. "Oh, I'm fine. Just a lot on my mind. I don't have work today by the way", I said. "Nice. I can go out to look for a job today. I'll just need a ride to the metro train station, if you don't mind", he asked. "Sure, I'll shower and get ready to go see a friend", I said still looking at the room door.

My HIV status hit me like a ton of bricks. I had to tell Tyler. I would have to tell him when the time was right. My status is not publically known and I would hate for him to leave now and go tell the world. I would have to build trust between us, even if there was lots of sexual chemistry between us.

After dropping Tyler off at the nearest metro train station, I called Amanda and we decided to go out for lunch. I just really wanted to talk to someone who understood what I was going through. I was feeling trapped in my guilt for leaving Alan and wanted to grieve. During lunch Amanda and I both set there crying our eyes out. Since there will be no memorial service I wanted to find a way for me to remember Alan. ..

Even though Amanda and I were very close, I hesitated to tell her about Tyler. She's never heard me talk about him and now he's living with me. Hell, I only just met him days ago. I wasn't exactly sure what I was doing with my life at that moment. I just allowed a stranger to stay with me. Even though deep down I felt like he really needed my help at that time in his life, I didn't want to get too attached to Tyler.

After about a week of looking, Tyler was offered a job at a pizza place close to my apartment. This worked out well for him since it was close to where we were living. After seeing Tyler work so hard at the pizza place I decided to pay for his modeling classes at the Trusey Agency. The classes were actually very expensive and was about a quarter of my monthly salary. I wanted to really see him make his dreams a reality, so I would give him extra pointers. I knew that Mark thought Tyler had great potential so I looked at me paying his fees as an investment for both our futures. By this time our relationship had grown very quickly.

Even though there's lots of sexual chemistry between us I've been able to tame it. I told him I don't have sex with anyone until at least two months of getting to know them. Even though he would still try I can tell he respected my rules. I was only trying to buy time to tell him about my status. One day just out of the blue he came right out and asked me, "Would you date someone who was HIV positive". "I would. I would just have to be careful. Why did you ask me that", I asked him as if I knew he had found out somehow. "I was just wondering. I would also. It would be hard but I think if we both were careful then it would work out", he said. Feeling like this was the perfect time and my moment to get it out; I just did without taking another breath. "Tyler, I'm HIV positive", I said so quickly that he didn't understand what I said. "What? What did you say", he asked. "I'm HIV positive", I said slowly. "Whoa. Are you serious? Or, are you just saying that because I just asked you that", he asked. I turned to look him dead in the eyes, "no, I'm serious. I've been waiting on a good time to tell you. That's one of the reasons why I don't want us to have sex", I said. "Wow. I'm sorry to hear that. If there's anything I can do please let me know", he said slowly. "It's not a death sentence. It's not like I'm going to just drop dead. I take my meds, and I eat really healthy", I said as he grabbed each side of my face giving me a deep heated passionate kiss. From there we indulged in each other as if we've anticipating doing for a long time. Even though I was the top in my relationship with Alan, Tyler had a natural dominance that I could only surrender to. The gentle way he bit my neck gave me a high that I can barely explain. My body released all tension and melted into his touches. No one has ever made me feel the way Tyler did. I was in love again. Tyler was perfect.

The next day I went to work and enrolled Tyler into classes with The Trusey Agency. Mark was able to guarantee all of his students work after they graduated his three month course.

His students had class twice a week for those three months. Even though his classes were expensive lots of people wanted to attend them. They knew Mark's work and trusted his leadership. I also trusted his work hence is why I've been working for him for years. He knew the business and he knew modeling. Through the three months his students will learn everything from camera angles to the runway. Since I worked the reception desk it was one of my responsibilities to accept payments from the students every month as they arrived for classes. I was able to pay Tyler's tuition without Mark knowing. I didn't want to tell Mark about Tyler and me, because I didn't want there to be any conflicts of interest between any of us. Mark was a mentor to me and I just didn't want him that close to my personal affairs. I still haven't told him about my status. I'm afraid of how he would react to it. He's always told me stories of people he knew back in his day that has died from AIDS and I would hate for him to become scared for me. My status is something I still haven't totally come to grips with. I don't plan on telling anyone else. I just plan on taking good care of myself and hopefully I would live long.

LANCE VII

After about a month and a half, I was finally offered several modeling gigs. Since I haven't been modeling for months at that point I immediately began to hit the gym every day, just to make sure my body stayed right for the shoots. A couple of the shoots were for a new urban clothing store that was in the process of opening in Atlanta. Mark also landed me on Runway Stars. Runway Stars was an annual majorly broadcasted runway fashion show. All the top brands and celebrities came out to this event. Even though this was a one night event, I was booked to be in New York for five days. The first few days I was booked to do promo work and rehearsals for Runway Stars. Since the event was to take place out in New York, I would have to leave Tyler by himself for the first time in Atlanta. Tyler and I have grown extremely close, I totally trusted him with everything. Since he would have to make it to class, I decided to leave him my car also so that he could drop me off and pick me up at the airport.

The money Tyler made from the pizza place was good enough to pay his phone bill, and to save a bit. I didn't ask him to pay rent because I really wanted to help him get on his feet. Since we were now in a serious relationship, I would have felt bad for asking him to pay rent anyway.

Tyler says he barely has any family. He told me that he has a brother, that's in prison for life, for murdering his dad. He also says that he doesn't speak to his mom. He says that she was a drug addict that caused him lots of pain and embarrassment as a child. He also says he's actually from Texas but was living in Las Vegas recently with friends. To be a part of Tyler's life felt like a pleasure. I wanted to be the person who meant something to him in his life.

Being in New York was great. I've done lots of work there before and plus I had plenty of friends I've met throughout the years that was going to be there for the event. The whole time I was in New York, Tyler called and texted constantly just to let me know he was thinking of me. He really made me feel special.

The night of Runway Stars, I went out with some of the other models to an after party. Before I went to the club I tried to call Tyler but I didn't get an answer. This was the first time I have ever called him and not gotten an answer. I thought that maybe he was sleep, in the shower, etc., even though it was only 11pm in New York, meaning that it was only 10pm in Atlanta. Tyler is a night owl, he stays up until at least 3am every night. The whole night while I was at the after party, I looked at my phone to see if Tyler tried to call me back, but no, I got nothing. I tried to text him and still didn't hear back from him that night.

The next day I was set to fly back to Atlanta. When I woke up I had a text from Tyler. He says that he fell asleep early last night and assured that he was going to be at the airport to pick me up at 8pm. I called him immediately after reading the text. "Is everything okay? I was worried about you ", I said as soon as he answered. "Yes, babe. Everything is good. I'm so sorry I missed your call. My phone has been acting up", he said non-chalantly. "Did you go to sleep early, or was your phone acting up", I asked. "I fell asleep early. I ended up working a double shift last night. I dropped my phone while I was at work yesterday. I'm sorry I missed your call baby", he said sincerely. "Oh, it's okay. I was just worried" I said. In my mind I felt like something wasn't right, but in my heart I wanted to believe what Tyler was saying.

As soon as my plane landed in Atlanta at 7:59pm, I called Tyler to make sure he was on his way to pick me up. I called three times back to back but he didn't answer. I even texted him where he was and didn't get a response. I had began to get really angry. If there was one thing I hated, that was waiting for people, especially at Atlanta's busy airport. When I got off the plane I immediately headed to baggage claim, which took at least twenty minutes. The whole time, I was still calling Tyler with no answer. After about thirty minutes of waiting and getting pissed he finally called me. "Where are you and why aren't you answering your phone", I said angrily. "Babe, I'm so sorry you know my phone isn't acting right. I'm on my way, I should be there in about twenty minutes", he said. "Twenty minutes? Are you serious? You were supposed to be here almost an hour ago", I said angrily. "I lost track of time baby. I know you're upset. Like I said I'll be there in about twenty minutes. I'll pick you up in the front at Arrivals", he said. "Hurry up", I said as I hung up the phone.

I walked outside the airport and set on a concrete stomp watching other travelers greet their families and partners as they arrived. I got so pissed sitting there. The more and more I waited, the more I was starting to doubt Tyler. He's never seemed so irresponsible before. Twenty minutes turned into two more hours of me sitting there, waiting for him to arrive. 11:03pm there's only me and a security guard standing outside as Tyler finally pulls up. My face was so tight. I could only see red. I couldn't believe he had me waiting for three hours. "What the fuck have you been doing", I asked as I opened the passenger side door to get in. "Babe, I know you're really upset. I got lost trying to get here. I took the wrong way on 285 and ended up going all the way around Atlanta", he said remorsefully. "Why didn't you call and say that?! I could have told you how to get here from my apartment", I said. "I'm going to get another phone tomorrow. See look", he said as he handed me his phone which had a huge crack through the screen. "Tyler, just don't ever let this happen again. I really hate waiting" I said demandingly. He then unbuckled his seat belt and reached over to grab my face to give me a kiss. Damn his kisses were so good; I seriously forgot why I was upset as his soft moist lips touched mine. He re-buckled his seat belt, put the car in drive and we were on our way home.

When we got back to my apartment, I was so exhausted I just wanted to get in bed and get some rest. I went into the kitchen to get a glass of water to take my medication, to find dirty plates and cups in the sink, two pizza boxes stuffed on top of an already filled garbage can. Tyler was not the "clean up" type of guy, which I quickly grew to understand. When I got into bed and pulled back the covers, I was a bit puzzled to see that Tyler had changed the sheets since I've left. I've only been gone for a few days. Tyler never does laundry; I'm always changing the sheets and washing them. "So you decided to change the sheets", I asked. "Oh yes, I was trying to make sure you came home to a clean home, that's all", he said as he took off his shirt. I then noticed four light scratches on his lower back. "Oh okay, thanks", I said. How did he think to change the sheets, but didn't think to wash the dirty dishes in the sink? After lying in bed for about five minutes, Tyler cuddled up behind me. I definitely wasn't in the mood for anything and he didn't even try to make a move. I can tell he felt my uncertainty.

The next morning, we decided to go to the nearest phone store to replace Tyler's broken phone. Even though Tyler's story seemed to add up, I still felt like something wasn't right.

Later that evening while we both set in the living room watching TV, Tyler fell asleep on the couch with his phone on the arm rest. I grabbed his new phone just to see if I could find anything suspicious. I did just that. I found a text message from a number that was not saved into his phone, in which I understood since he just got a new phone that day. The message said, "Why did you have to leave so suddenly last night? I was really enjoying you". My heart began to race because he never mentioned going anywhere last night. Wherever he went is the reason why he was three hours late picking me up from the airport.

After reading the message, I looked at him while he was sleeping and I wanted punch him in the face as he slept. I quickly calmed myself and decided I would call the unsaved number from my own cell phone. As I'm dialing the number my phone begins to automatically suggest numbers like the one I'm dialing. The more numbers I dialed, the more my phone automatically eliminated its suggested contacts. As I type in the last and final number, the only contact that's left is Mark's. It was Mark's number. Tyler had been hanging out with Mark last night. I couldn't believe this. I quietly put his phone back on the arm rest. I went to my bed room, just to get some air and to calm down before I made any bad decisions. I wanted to fight him. I couldn't be mad at Mark because Mark didn't know of Tyler and I. Or maybe he did now, since Tyler apparently has been driving my car around Mark. Before I left we discussed that Mark is not to know about our relationship. When he goes to classes he's suppose to park in the parking garage down the street from the agency, so that no one sees him driving my car and begins to suspects anything. Now I'm feeling like Mark knows everything and he's sleeping with Tyler.

Later that night when Tyler woke up, I was in the bedroom lying in bed. He jumped on the bed and laid on top of me trying to grind on me. I quickly turned around and pushed him off me. "Do you think I'm fuckin' stupid", I said angrily. "Whoa. What did I do", he asked as he set up in the bed. "Where were you last night? Don't give me no bullshit because I already know", I said. "Know what?! What do you know", he asked loudly. "I know you were with Mark. Are you fucking him" I asked. "No, no, no. Absolutely not. I'm so sorry Lance", he said as he stood up to his feet to face me. "I was trying to surprise you with some extra money. Mark has a friend that had a bachelorette party last night. He asked me after class one day, if I would be interested in making some extra money dancing at his friends' party. I told him yes. I went and danced at the party last night. Mark asked me to stay even later at the party but I had to pick you up. I didn't want to tell you because I didn't think you'd understand. I figured I could help you pay some rent", he explained. I felt stupid. I felt like I was over reacting. "Tyler, is there anything else that I should know. You have to communicate those things to me, so that I'll know. I understand if you wanted to make some extra money, but you could have told me that. Please never keep anything else from me. I'm in this for you and I", I said feeling a bit guilty. I felt relieved because this explains the four light scratches on his side. I was thinking then that one of the ladies must have scratched him, while he gave her a lap dance. "Lance, there's something else I want to admit to you", he said. "What's that", I replied expecting to hear the worse. "I love you", he said as he climbed on top of me kissing me and forcing me on my back. Feeling so overwhelmed I began to exhale and allowed my tears to flow as Tyler kissed, nibbled, licked, and entered my body. Once again Tyler was perfect.

Tyler had become exactly what I've needed in a partner. He was more concerned about me taking my meds than I was. After we would come back from the gym or even a light jog he would run me warm baths and massage my entire body. He began cooking very healthy meals for the both of us. I swore Tyler was an angel, sent to me by God.

LANCE VIII

A few weeks had passed when Mark called me into his office. "So how's my star model", he asked. I can tell by his voice, he was about to ask me a favor that he hoped I'd say yes to. "What is it Mark? Your "star model" needs some "star" work", I said jokingly. "I know and you're going to start getting busier very soon. I need you back in the gym heavily. There's a few lines getting ready to shoot their Spring catalogs, and I'm going to get you in a few of those. I've also gotten you another shoot next week for The HIV Foundation", he said slowly hoping that I'll agree. I got instantly nervous because Mark must have somehow found out about my status. The only person that could have told him was Tyler. I paused staring at Mark. "How did you find out about my status", I asked quickly with a straight face. "What?! No, Lance. What?! Your status?! Hold on Lance, what are you saying...?", he asked. I knew then that I spoke way too quickly. I closed my eyes taking a deep breath. "Lance, are you saying you are HIV positive? I didn't know that... I was just trying to get you more work", he said.

"I'm so sorry Mark. I am HIV positive. I, I, I didn't want you to find out like this, but yes", I said. "No, don't be sorry son. I feel like crap because I should have known this", he said. "There's no way you could have known. I haven't told anyone", I said trying to build up a smile. "Wow, Lance I'm lost for words, I don't know what else to say", he said confused. "There's nothing to say. I'll do the shoot", I said. "You're such a strong person Lance. If there is anything I can do for you, please let me know", he said as he got up from his desk to come around to give me a hug. "I love you Lance. You're like a son to me. Now… is there anything else about you that I need to know", he asked smiling and laughing. "I love you too Mark. Well… Do you know your student Tyler? Well… I've been seeing him for the last few months", I said looking down. "Oh, that's old news. I knew that already. I've been waiting on you to tell me about it. By the way, stop letting that boy drive your car", he said laughing while he opened his office door for us to walk out.

Mark and I used to be very close. Now I felt us get even closer. I can't believe he knew all along about Tyler and I. The thought of that made me laugh to myself. It felt good to not have to hide my relationship with Tyler.

When the day of the HIV Foundation shoot arrived, I was extremely nervous about it. Even though I've been prepped by the foundations owners. I still wasn't comfortable with my status enough to do a whole shoot about it. This shoot was a half naked shoot, with the red HIV ribbon painted across my chest. Even though I was a bit ashamed, doing this shoot really empowered me. I began to think of how many lives I could save. As I'm shooting I began to think that I could use my little modeling celebrity to raise more awareness about HIV/AIDS. With every shoot the photographer snapped I felt my strength building. After the shoot was done, I went over to the foundations' owner. I shook his hand and I told him that I would love the opportunity to be a spokesperson for his foundation. "Wow, Lance I would love that. I've always admired your work in modeling, and I know I could use your help. I have a commercial that we will be shooting soon for the foundation. I would love for you to take the lead role on that one" he explained. "Sure, that sounds awesome. I believe in your cause and I just want to help other people out there", I said. "So I have to ask, besides just modeling, what makes you interested in the HIV Foundation", he asked. "Well... I am HIV positive myself and I want to help other people", I said boldly. It felt so good to be able to be honest about my status to a complete stranger. The more I spoke about it, the better I felt. As I told him I was HIV positive his eyes opened wide in surprise. "Wow. I didn't know that. How are you doing? I mean, if you don't mind me asking", he said. "No problem. I have my days, but for the most part I feel good. I eat right and take my meds" I said. "Absolutely. That's all we can do, plus pray" he said. From there we talked for about another thirty minutes about his future plans for the foundation.

When I got home that night I was greeted at the door by Tyler with a long stemmed red rose in his mouth. He grabbed me by the middle of my shirt pulling me closer to him. He kissed the rose from his mouth to mine. "What is this about? What is that you're cooking that smells so good", I asked taking the rose out of my mouth. "I'm proud of you. I'm proud of us. So I decided to cook your favorite, lasagna. Mark says that I'm ready to start being booked for modeling gigs. He has already got me a shoot with The Doll House Magazine, next week in Los Angeles", he said excitedly. "Wow. That's awesome! The Doll House is huge! I wanted to do The Doll House", I said. The Doll House magazine is a Bi-Monthly magazine for women that feature the sexiest of the sexiest men from around the world. It's a bit like Play Boy but they don't show genitalia. I knew then that this was going to be a big deal for Tyler's modeling career. There have been guys in this business for many years that have been trying to get in The Doll House Magazine. For this major opportunity to be his first shoot, I prayed that he stayed humble about it.

That night after we ate we cuddled on the couch. Tyler talked me to sleep about how excited he was about this opportunity. He whispered promises of a great future as he held me tightly through the night.

LANCE IX

The next week Tyler had left for Los Angeles for his first photo shoot. I was extremely proud of him. Since we'd been together for months at that point I had really trusted Tyler. The whole time he was in Los Angeles, he called me constantly just to check on me. By this time my health was up and down. One day I felt great, the next I felt like I was going to die. Having Tyler in my life gave me new purpose to exist. Even when I didn't feel too well, I would pretend to, so that he wouldn't worry.

Since Tyler was going to be out in LA for a few days, I took this time to hang out with Amanda. Surprisingly, I haven't seen her since around the time Alan died. She has since made excuses every time I invited her over to my apartment. I figured we could meet somewhere near her job. She invited me to a deli, which was right across the street from the cell phone business in which she worked. Seeing Amanda felt really refreshing, but I would admit that she didn't act like herself. Normally, when Amanda and I would hang out, we were both loud and crazy, but this time she was almost like a stranger. Normally, we could talk on and on for hours but she seemed very short with me. I asked her if everything was okay, she ensured me that things were good and that she was just tired from working so much lately. I wasn't sure what it was, but I could definitely tell it wasn't from working so much. I've spent lots of time with Amanda and this wasn't the "tired" Amanda. There was a lot on her mind and I could tell she was probably hiding something from me. "Amanda, you can't lie to your best friend. What is going on with you? I haven't seen you in lord knows how long and you're treating me like a stranger", I said. "Lance, of course I know that. I'm tired and I just found out I'm pregnant", she said slowly but angrily. "What?! Oh my God, I'm going to be an uncle?! That's awesome Amanda! I'm so happy for you", I said smiling. Amanda didn't crack a smile at all; she just stared at the ground. "I'm getting an abortion. I can't keep this baby", she said as she still stared at the ground. "Whoa. I think you should think about that twice. I'll be here for you. If you need anything you know you can count on me", I said. "Thanks Lance, but this is my body. I'm getting an abortion", she said firmly. "Hold up, what does your boyfriend think about this", I asked. "We broke up over a month ago. I don't think... Look, this is all new to me and I'm not feeling so well. Thanks for coming but I have to get back to work", she said quickly as she got up from the table and headed for the door. I didn't say anything back I just allowed her to walk out without a word. I couldn't believe what was going on in her life. As much as I was excited for her, I was also scared for her. As a friend, I understood and still wanted to at least be there for her.

The next day I picked Tyler up from the airport, "How was everything", I asked him as soon as he get into the car. Without a word and leaned over and gave me a kiss. "It was awesome now that I'm back in your presence", he said charmingly. He always seemed to know what to say and how. The rest of the day we just rented movies online and cuddled. The love I felt between Tyler and I was like no other. Everything in my life seemed right, whenever Tyler was present.

Since doing the shoot for The Doll House, Tyler's modeling career began to take off very fast. He had began to get offers from everywhere. Now that he was working, he did pay his half of the rent. Even though he had been living rent free, I didn't ask for him to pay me back for the months he wasn't able to pay. I didn't ask him to pay back the money I spent on his classes with Mark either. I was deeply in love and figured that it was all an investment into our future together.

LANCE X

Since Tyler was so busy with his new modeling career, I had begun to work a lot on the HIV Foundation. I was now a spokesperson for the foundation, so I would go around to different events in town to speak about HIV awareness. Working with the foundation was by far the most rewarding thing I've ever done in my life. It gave me a chance to give back. Talking with people about this disease, gave me lots of strength. Most of the people I would talk to were teenagers. I loved sharing my story and life with them. Knowing by sharing my story with them will help them make better life choices, meant the world to me.

In between that time, the foundation had decided to prepare to shoot a national commercial. Since I was now the spokesperson and a well known model, they asked me to be the lead in the commercial. This would be the first time my status will be nationally publicized. I wasn't nervous at all about that part, I knew what I was doing was going to help someone.

The day of the commercial shoot, I asked Tyler to come along with me on the shoot for moral support. Though he was a bit hesitant he ultimately agreed to tag along with me. When Tyler and I arrived to the commercial shoot, which was done in a television studio, I had began to feel a bit ill. I pretended as I've always done to feel good but I wasn't.

"Hey, Mr. Kirk! I'm here and ready to go", I said as we approached Mr. Kirk and the Director of the commercial. "My my my, it's my star Lance! How's it going? Do you have your lines memorized", Mr. Kirk asked me laughing and smiling. "Lance, this is the director of the commercial, Rick", Mr. Kirk said as I reached to shake Rick's hand. "This is my partner Tyler, he came to...", I had begin to say when Tyler cut me off. "I'm his friend... Tyler. I just came to support", Tyler said as he shook Mr. Kirk and Rick's hands. I was a bit saddened by how Tyler just degraded me down to being just his friend. We were indeed more than friends, but for some reason Tyler didn't want that to be known. I was a bit embarrassed but I went along as if it didn't bother me. After about six hours we were done shooting the Public Service Announcement for the HIV Foundation. Even though six hours isn't a long time I was drained. I was not only sick I was now hurt by Tyler's quick switch.

"So we're just friends now", I asked as we got in the car. "I knew you were going to bring that up. I just want to keep our personal lives private. I didn't think it was professional for them to know we were partners", he said. Though I would admit for a second I agreed with Tyler, because it did make some sense, but still... "Okay, I see but...", I said emotionlessly as I continued to drive. "But, what?! Lance you asked me to come along with you for moral support, not to be paraded around like a trophy piece", he said. "Are you serious right now", I asked looking at him not paying much attention to the road. "I'm dead serious. I'm not a fucking trophy piece. You just want everyone to know you're with me", he said. "Tyler. Firstly, please don't swear at me. You're crazy if you think I'm using you in that way", I said. "I'm not crazy. I see exactly what you're doing", he said. "What am I doing to you? I've done everything FOR you. Remember you were the one on the streets with no money and no place to live. I took you in", I said getting loud. "I've done more for you then you've done for me. You only wanted to take me in because your lonely, HIV infested ass couldn't find no one else to entertain what you were going through", he argued. I was shocked about what he had just said to me. I quickly pulled the car over and put it into park. "Tyler, whoa! How can you say that to me? Is that really how you feel? I thought you said you loved me? That's not love coming from your mouth", I said. "Love? Love is not how you tried to embarrass me today! You're a fucking joke. A sick fucking faggot", he said. I slapped him hard with the back of my right hand. He just turned and looked at me without saying a word. "I'm not going to let you disrespect me like that. I've done everything for YOU. If you had an issue with my status why did you stick around, I asked him angrily. "I'll fuck a sick bitch to get what I want... I'm out...", he said as he grabbed the door handle to get out of the car. At that instance, as if it was perfectly planned it had begun to rain. Tyler didn't seem to be phased by the rain as he walked away in front of my car. As my head lights lit his path through the dark rainy night, my heart wouldn't allow me to let him to walk in the rain. I picked him up in the rain and now... I got out of my car and ran behind him. "Tyler, listen. I'm sorry", I said as I walked closer behind him grabbing his right shoulder to turn him around. As he turned around he swung his fist hard into my face. The impact was so strong and unexpected that I couldn't brace myself. I fell to the wet gravel on the side of the street. He then stood over me and kick me hard in the abdomen and spit on me. "Stay the fuck away from me, faggot", he yelled. The kick to my abdomen was so hard that I could barely catch my breath. The rain was now coming down so hard when I tried to breathe in, I choked on the rain water.

After about 30 seconds I managed to get back to my feet. I was in rage; I couldn't believe or even clearly comprehend my current reality. Tyler just totally flipped out on me, but I was going to make him pay. My first thought was to have him fired from the agency so that he wouldn't get more work. As I slowly walked back to my car, holding my abdomen, I could see someone sitting in the passenger side. I quickly wiped the rain from my eye thinking that I was seeing things. It was Alan. He was sitting in the passenger seat just staring at me. Knowing what I was seeing couldn't be real I went to wipe my eyes again. This time when I looked at my car there was no one there. I figured my mind was playing tricks on me again.

I got into my car and quickly put it in drive. I was furious. I began to drive fast and about a minute of driving I could see Tyler walking on the side of the road. I drove quickly behind him and got closer and closer. The closer I got the more I wanted to kill him. I drove straight into him and continued to drive as his body flipped over my windshield. I didn't feel relieved. I was completely out of my mind. My first thought was that I just killed him. I knew I couldn't just leave him there so I made a quick U-turn. Hearing my tires squeal on the wet pavement made me feel like I was in a movie or something. I stopped the car right in front of Tyler as he lay motionless in the street. I stared at him for a few seconds, thinking... how did this all just happen.

I quickly got out of the car and ran to his side. Blood was rushing from his face. I tried to shake his body but he wasn't responding. "No, No, No, wake up. Tyler I'm sorry, please wake up", I cried as I seen another car about 300 feet away coming toward the scene. I quickly thought to take Tyler's wallet and phone from his pockets. I was trying to think quickly of how not to trace Tyler back to me. I quickly figured if he had nothing on him they would have a hard time identifying him. The other car's headlights were so bright that I fell into a quick daze just staring at them. "Is everything okay? Sir, are you okay? Sir? Did you hit someone? Is he breathing?", a strong voice called to me but I couldn't find the means to respond. I felt like I was living the bad part of a dream and I was waiting for myself to wake up. When I finally came to, I quickly stood up and said, "I was driving and he just came out of now where. I don't think he's breathing." In an instance I decided I would lie about knowing Tyler at all. "Have you called the police", the strong masculine voice asked me. "No, please call the police", I said stuttering. I was frantic. I just killed Tyler and I knew I would go to jail for this. As the guy called the police I began to see he was a middle aged, short, chubby, white guy. He wore a red flannel shirt and a baseball cap. He looked like a truck driver.

As I turned away to look back at my car I noticed a huge dent on the hood. I scanned up to look at the windshield, when I seen Alan again sitting in the passenger side. He looked back at me with a deep stare as if he was looking through me. He raised his left hand holding a gun. He placed the gun barrel on the side of his head and slowly began to pull the trigger. "Noooo", I screamed looking away covering my eyes as if I was a kid watching a scary movie. "Are you okay? The police is on their way", the man said to me. I couldn't say anything, I was in total shock. The guy kneeled down to Tyler to check his pulse. "He's still alive! He has a pulse, very faint but he has one at least", the man said looking up at me. I just looked back at him crying and sobbing.

Moments later three police cars and an ambulance arrived. The paramedics immediately rushed to Tyler's side. A policeman asked me to follow him back to his car to get out of the rain. I was still crying and I knew I was going to jail for this. He opened the backseat door and told me to get in. He got in the front seat and told me that he need to get a report from me of what happened. I stuck with my lie. I told the policeman that I was driving in the rain and he darted out in front of me. I knew with that information they couldn't charge me with a crime because at that time it appeared to be just an accident.

 In the short distance I could see the paramedics putting Tyler in the back of the ambulance. He wasn't covered with a white sheet, so I figured he must've been still alive. I felt relieved, but still troubled.

After talking to the policeman he told me that I was free to leave the scene. I went back to my car and began to cry. My eyes were so filled with tears that I decided to pull into a super market's parking lot, which was about three minutes from the scene. I sat there thinking hard about what I should do. I knew that if Tyler made a complete recovery that he would tell exactly what happened. I would be facing attempted murder charges; on top of that I lied to the police in my report. I could potentially be in prison for the rest of my life. As I set there with rain on my windshield and tears in my eyes Tyler's phone made a sound. I pulled the phone from my pocket and turned it on to find that the screen was cracked but I could still see the details on it. It was a text message from a number in which he didn't have saved in his phone. The text message said, "Did you tell him yet...". Since the number wasn't saved I decided to read through the text messages. I noticed he had been getting messages from this number all day. I scrolled to the beginning of where the messages started and noticed they started about a week ago. The conversation was started by Tyler:

Tyler: Hey!

Unknown Number: Hey, who is this.

Tyler: It's Tyler. I got your number from his phone...

Unknown Number: Oh! Hey! What's up?

Tyler: Nothing much just working...

I didn't know who he was referring to when he said "his phone". I then scrolled further down and seen

Unknown Number: I'm pregnant.

Tyler: Congrats to you and your boyfriend!

Unknown Number: We never got back together... I haven't had sex with him in months. You were the last person I had sex with.

Tyler: No. You're not going to pin that thing on me.

Unknown Number: You didn't mind "pinning" me down to Lance's bed! You need to tell Lance. If you don't I will...

I was in total shock at it all. These messages were the icing on the cake to my moments of insanity. To clarify I had began to dial the unknown number into my phone and seen that it was indeed Amanda. In my moment of fury, I pressed the call button and waited a few seconds as my phone called Amanda. As soon as she said "Hello", I blurted with all emotions "WHY DID YOU DO THIS TO ME". I threw my phone down on the passenger seat, put the car in drive and began and slammed on the gas. "Hello, Lance I'm so sorry, I'm so sorry. Lance, Lance.." I heard coming from the phone. As I began to drive, I could feel a presence in the car with me. I could still hear Amanda on the phone "Lance... Lance... I'm so sorry". When I looked back down at my phone in the passenger side there was Alan sitting there. He stared at me emotionlessly without blinking. I was truly losing my mind. I turned to look at the street where I was now driving to hopefully shake the illusion of Alan, but when I turned back he was still there just staring. I could still here Amanda on the phone apologizing. As

Amanda is saying "I'm sorry, I'm so sorry", on the phone, I had began to scream "I'M SORRY ALAN, PLEASE GO AWAY". As I said that, he turned his head and eyes from me to look in front at the highway. He just stared straight ahead. In those few quick moments I quickly turned my head and attention back to the street. Right in front of me was a stopped semi truck and I had no time to react...

THE B Y
CHRONICLES

TYLER
SMITS

Birthday: May 20
Sign: Gemini
Occupation: Convicted Felon / Model
Education: 11th Grade
Personality Type: Charismatic, Mystique, Ambitious, Rebellious

TYLER

"I don't remember getting hit by a car. The last thing I remember is walking in the rain. It all must've happened so fast because I didn't feel a thing. The next thing I knew was a doctor waking me up in this hospital and now my ankle is broken", I said to the detective. "From what we've gathered it seems as if the guy that hit you also robbed you. We found your cell phone and wallet in the wreckage", the detective said. "What wreckage", I asked. "The guy that hit you was killed in a terrible accident last night. I guess it was just a bad case of Karma", the detective said. He continued to talk after that but I couldn't focus clearly. My mind had gone into shock but weirdly I wasn't sad about the news I had just received. I was actually relieved and bit happy he was dead. As the detective continued to talk, I slipped into a long day dream about how I even gotten to this point...

TYLER I

I had just moved to Atlanta from Las Vegas with a friend named Rob that I met on Craigslist. He was looking for a roommate and I was looking for a place to stay. My life in Las Vegas had gotten extremely hectic and I needed a change in scenery. I had recently been released from jail for robbery and drug possession. In life most would and could say that I was a failure. I was adopted as a baby by a woman who had three other children. We grew up in the Catholic Church, where I was molested by a priest from the age of 8 to 13, when I finally had the strength to say something about it, my adopted family didn't believe me and labeled be a liar. Around that same time, my mother admitted to me that I was adopted. I resented her, the family, every part of the Catholic Church, and my real parents, whom which I never knew. I had begun to act up so much that I ended up in a couple detention centers as a teenager. When I was 17, I finally went to jail for the first time for grand theft and since then my adopted family has stopped communicating with me. I've made several attempts to try to find them but all have been unsuccessful. I never finished high school and I quit everything I've ever started.

Going to Atlanta would allow me to go to a new place where no one knew me. I thought I could possibly begin to turn my life around for the better. Rob helped me land a little bartending job at a gay night club called, "Tricks". Working at Tricks was a nice way for me to make a little money to help pay my part of the rent. Still feeling a bit frustrated about my living situation, I wanted more from life. I didn't know how or where but I knew I no longer wanted to be a loser.

Working at Tricks I received a lot of compliments from the gay guys that would come into the club. They would often ask me if I modeled. I thought they were just trying to flirt with me. I had never been with a guy before so I would admit that their compliments made me uncomfortable. I figured since I had gotten so much attention from the gay guys here in Atlanta, I should find a good one to hook up with. I've heard many times that gay guys are normally very vulnerable and easy. Just showing a gay guy a little love and affection will enable me to have all that I wanted from him. Gay guys are usually extremely superficial and don't mind paying. I was going to use all that I knew to get what I wanted.

One night a guy came into the night club trying to flirt with me and I paid it no mind. I overheard him talking to another guy at the bar about his relationship. He told the other guy that his boyfriend was Lance Calloway, a famous model. He went on and on, saying how Lance had broken his heart. From behind the bar I quickly grabbed a piece of paper and wrote down "Lance Calloway". My plan was for me to look him up, to see if I could possibly find out which company he worked for here in Atlanta. Since I knew nothing about modeling, I figured I'd start there. I was going to come up with a plan to financially better myself. I knew by then, it wasn't about what you know but who you know. As soon as I wrote down his name, I was side tracked by someone trying to order a drink. I slid the small slip of paper in one of the pockets of my bar apron. I forgot about looking him up, until Alan returned to the night club about a week later trying to fight the guy he was talking with from before. After work that night I decided to "Google", "Lance Calloway". I saw that he was indeed a well-known model that was signed to the Trusey Agency in Atlanta. I also did research on the "Trusey Agency" and seen that they were actually looking for new models. I felt like this could be my chance to finally begin my way to the top. I have never considered modeling but if the gay guys thought I could, I was willing to give it a try.

I went to the Trusey Agency, where I unexpectedly met Lance. I was really surprised to see him there in person. I felt very timid and a bit star struck at first. I left the agency the first day feeling a bit uncertain about modeling. The agency's owner Mark Trusey, told me that I would need to take some classes from him; that I honestly couldn't afford. Since this was a legit agency and situation, I wanted to make sure I stayed around because as I said; it's not what you know, it's who you know. The next time I saw Lance, I was prepared with my own plan. I had planned that I would do whatever it takes to be part of his life. I was going to make him fall for me.

At that point, my roommate Rob had been evicted from his apartment for not paying the rent. Even though I was giving him my part of the rent he wasn't paying it. Since my name wasn't on the lease I had to go as well. This caused a physical altercation between Rob and I, which led to absolutely nothing. He had no explanation for what he did with my part of the rent. I really had no place to go and I quickly became desperate. I played on Lances' emotions. I knew way more about him than he thought I knew. I knew his ex-boyfriend Alan had died even before he found out from the news, that day at the Trusey Agency. I knew he would be extremely vulnerable and emotional so I put my game and plans in motion. I wanted to get what he had plus more. I was sick and tired of being broke and useless. I wheeled him in with my charm. I told him everything he wanted to hear. When he told me he was HIV positive, I wasn't too shocked because I had already knew. I snooped through his bedroom drawers and seen the medication he was taking. I researched the medications and realized it was medication for people who was HIV positive. I made him feel secure with me. I embraced him when he finally told me his status because I knew that would make him fall for me faster. I knew that I would have to be extra careful when it came to sex with him. I had already researched ways on how to have sex with someone who was HIV positive and how not to become infected. Of course, the popular answer was to use condoms. I knew Lance was going to be my way into much success and I was willing to risk my own life for it.

One night while Lance was out of town, there was frantic knock at the door. When I opened the door the girl who I later learned was Amanda, was crying and asking to speak to Lance. She told me that she and Lance were like sister and brother, even though they haven't spoken at that point in weeks. I told her, he was out of town but I was willing to help her with what she was going through. She was telling me that her boyfriend had just broken up with her and she really needed a place to stay for that night. We ended up talking for hours that night over a bottle of wine. The more we talked the closer we had gotten. We decided to go to the bedroom and lay in Lance's bed. She asked me what was my involvement with Lance and I told her that we were in a relationship. I figured I should keep my plan in motion even with her. As we lay in the bed she crawled over and laid her head on my lower abdomen. I began to stroke my fingers through her hair. I became erect and wanted a piece of Amanda. It had been a long while since I had felt the touch of a woman and Amanda was super sexy. I actually hoped for that moment, the moment she walked in. The more I stroked her hair the bigger my erection became.

She was then laying on it when she turned her head and reached down my shorts pulling it out. She proceeded to lick and kiss it slowly. I knew what we were doing was wrong but it had been a long while since I touched a woman. She didn't seem to care and neither did I. In the heat of the moment and my desperate need to feel the insides of a woman again, led me into her body unprotected. I just didn't care, I was finding for her forbidden fruit.

When she left that night, we vowed to never speak of what had just took place. The next morning I woke up in bed, just thinking. The smell of Cucumber and Melons was melted into the sheets from Amanda's body. I rose up in bed and realized that strands of her hair were throughout the sheets. I immediately jumped up and put the sheets into the washer. I was going to get rid of all evidence before Lance could find out.

While Lance was out of town in New York, I cheated a few times. Even the night I had to pick him up from the airport. Even though I did have a side gig that night to make some extra money, I ended up having sex with one of the women from the party in Lance's car. I was great at pretending to be sincere to him. Part of me felt like I was paying him back for what he had done in his previous relationship. Even though I didn't know Alan much, I would justify my wrong with his pain. Karma is definitely a bitch and I was helping her do her job.

The night of Lance's death was by far the worst day of my life. Earlier that day while Lance was shooting his commercial I received several calls from Amanda. I didn't answer because I couldn't imagine why she would want to speak to me. What we had done was now the past and I wasn't going to let that interfere with my plans for the future. She then texted me and I thought that I should at least reply to her text messages. She eventually told me that she was pregnant and that I was the one who did it. Deep down I knew there was a possibility that it was definitely true, I still denied it. She threatened to tell Lance the truth and I couldn't bare that. I was infuriated. I could only see all that I planned being washed away. I was thinking to find a way to kill Amanda but it would take lots of planning.

Throughout that day my mood had shifted badly. I didn't mean to take it out on Lance but I didn't know how to deal with what was about to happen. I was already living a lie and this was going to be too much to keep up with.

When Lance had begun to question me that day, I didn't know how to handle it. I just wanted out. I had flipped out on him and made him my enemy. I knew what I was doing would eventually hurt him, but I didn't care. I was madder at the fact that I didn't have time for my full plan to follow through...

TYLER II

The doctors at the hospital told me that I was lucky to be alive. I only had a broken ankle, a deep cut on my face, and a few scrapes and bruises. When I was hit by the car my entire left leg was snapped out of socket from my hip. The doctors were able to pop in back into place while I was still unconscious. After two days had passed the doctors at the hospital told me that I was well enough to go home. The problem that haunted me the most was that I didn't have a home to go to. They placed a brace on my ankle and wrote me a strong prescription of pain pills that I would have to take for six weeks. I called a cab to pick me up from the hospital and to take me to the nearest pharmacy to retrieve my prescription. I went to a cheap hotel that night to have a place to stay. When I got to my room I took my medication and began to think up another plan.

The only other person that I knew in Atlanta was Mark, and I'm sure by that time he had heard parts of what was going on. I wasn't exactly sure how he may have felt over the death of Lance. I knew that Lance was almost like a son to him, which made me afraid to contact him. Since I was indeed signed to the Trusey Agency, I felt like I should at least reach out to Mark regarding work.

After being in the hotel for a couple days I decided to go out to purchase a new phone to call Mark. I called Mark but only received his voice mail. I left him several messages telling him that I was doing okay, and where to reach me. I wondered; why hasn't Mark tried to reach out to me? At that time, I was one of his top models for his agency. I would think he would want to know how I was doing.

Later that night I received a call back from Mark. I was excited to talk with him. Even though I had stitches in my face and a broken ankle, I wanted to know when I could get back to work to make more money. As soon as I said hello, Mark told me that he has terminated my contract. He didn't ask me how I was doing or made any mention of Lance. His excuse was that he felt like the Trusey Agency could no longer get me the modeling gigs that would benefit me or the agency. I knew what Mark had said was a bunch of crap. I didn't question him at all, I said "thank you" and hung up the phone. This made me furious. I couldn't put together in my mind what Mark could have possibly been told about my situation with Lance. I'm not sure what he knows, or who may have told him what he think he knows.

The next day I decided to book a flight and head back out to Las Vegas, in a week. I wanted to heal a bit and get the stitches out of my face before I went to Las Vegas. I figured my time in Atlanta was over and I needed to move on before things got any worse. I would use any experience and exposure I was able to gain from working with the Trusey Agency to find more work in Las Vegas. Since I had now been in magazines I thought it shouldn't be too hard to find work.

TYLER III

After my week in Atlanta, I was off to Las Vegas. As my plane landed in Las Vegas I felt a rush of refreshing energy run through my veins. I felt a new start was about to happen. The only person's phone number that I could remember was my old friend Britney. I called her Brit for short. She was just an average looking blond white girl. We actually used to date years back, but we decided that we were better friends than lovers. I hadn't heard from Brit in over a year, so I was sure she would be surprised to hear from me. Her phone rang about six times before she finally answered. "Hello", she answered confused. She was probably confused because I was calling from an Atlanta phone number. "Brit it's me", I said excited. "Who is me", she asked. "Me, Tyler. Your old friend, Tyler", I said laughing. "Tyler!? Tyler, I'm going to kick your ass! Where in the hell have you been", she asked excited. "I've been living in Atlanta for a while but I'm moving back home to Vegas", I said. "Dude, this is insane! I can't believe I'm speaking to you. I have seen your picture in magazines and everything. I didn't know you were a model", she said. "Yes,

I've been a busy man. I've come back to Vegas to further my career. We should meet up somewhere for dinner tonight", I proposed. "Yes, we should. Name the place and time, I will be there" she said excitedly. *"Jerry's House of Pork and Lanes*, at 8 o'clock", I asked. "Sure, I will be there", she said as we said our good byes.

Jerry's House of Pork and Lanes is a restaurant where we always go to hang out on the weekends, which was only about ten minutes from the airport. There was an arcade and bowling alley in the back of the restaurant.

After I hung up with Britney, I exited the plane, grabbed my luggage from baggage claim and took a cab to the cheapest and nearest hotel. I had planned to stay at the hotel only for a couple nights until I could find a place to stay.

I got to the restaurant and waited inside for about ten minutes before Britney had arrived. Seeing Britney was like heaven to me. It felt good to see a familiar face, after what I had just been through in Atlanta. I walked over and gave her a hug when the first thing she said to me was, "what happened to your face, and what's up with this limp in your walk". I told her that I was in a car wreck in Atlanta. I didn't tell her all the details though. We talked on and on for what seemed like hours. The more we talked the more comfortable I became. I eventually became comfortable enough to explain to her that I was now homeless and needed a place to stay, especially in my condition. She told me that she shares an apartment with her current boyfriend, and that I could sleep on her couch for a few days. We left the restaurant and she drove me to the hotel to get my things.

We went back to her apartment which was about 20 minutes away. I walked into her small apartment and knew immediately that I could only stay there for only a night. It was very small and messy. There were clothes and dirty dishes everywhere. "Find you a spot and get comfortable, I'll take your luggage to my room", Britney said as she grabbed my suitcase from my hand. Looking a bit uncertain I slid a dirty pair of white socks, and men underwear to the side and took a seat on the couch. "Where's your boyfriend? Will he be okay with me staying here", I asked. "Melvin, will be fine. He's at work and doesn't get off until after midnight", she assured me. She came back into the living room area and picked up the television remote from the cluttered sticky looking table. "You'll have to excuse my messy apartment. We are barely home together. I work during the days and Melvin begins work in the evening. We rarely have time to clean up", she explained as she turned on the television. "Oh ok, no problem", I replied. I really appreciated her for allowing me to stay so I wasn't going to complain.

We set in their living room watching television and waiting for her boyfriend to get home. She wanted to introduce us before she went off to bed. Around 12:30am Melvin walks into the apartment. Melvin is Hispanic. He's about 5'7, dark hair, full mustache and goatee. Very attractive. Britney quickly stood up and introduced us both to each other. I reached out my hand to shake his hand. He seemed to be very nice. Britney explained to him that I had just moved back to Vegas from Atlanta, and I needed a place to stay for a little while. "Do I know you from somewhere", Melvin asked me. "I don't think we have ever met", I said. "Well you may have seen him on a few billboards or something. He's a big time model now", Britney laughed. "Oh yea, that's probably where", Melvin laughed. I laughed along but didn't find any humor in the conversation. "Well, I'm off to bed now. I have to be at work at 7am. Good night boys", Britney said as she walked into the other room.

"Do you watch the basketball games at all", Melvin asked as he grabbed the remote and changed the channel. "Every now and then but I haven't lately. Who's your favorite team", I asked him. "Lakers. I love the Lakers. I've been a Lakers fan my entire life", he said. "Nice. I don't have a favorite. I just like watching", I said. We talked on and on about sports until I dozed off to sleep.

I woke up the next morning in lots of pain from my leg and ankle. I had it propped up on the arm of the couch, as I lay on my back. I got up slowly looking around to remember where I was. The television was still on, but I was in the living room alone. I grabbed my phone from the coffee table to check the time and it was 8:06am. I figured that Britney had already left for work. I rose from the couch and quietly limped to Britney's room to retrieve my medication, in which I had left in my luggage. Her bedroom door was cracked, so I slowly opened it as it made a softly screeching sound. I was a bit stunned to see Melvin lying on the left side of the bed with his entire naked backside out. Stunned, I quickly turned my head to look away. I figured he was just sleeping and I really needed to get to those pain pills. I spotted my suitcase sitting against a closet door that was on the right side of the bed. I walked over and grabbed my suitcase and limped out quickly.

When I got back to the living room, I opened my suitcase to get my medication out. I opened the pill bottle and shook out two 500mg Hydrocodone pills. I was in so much pain that I felt like I really needed it. I went to the kitchen to get some water but I couldn't find a clean cup. I limped back to the living room and grabbed a dirty cup from the coffee table and washed it out. I took my medication quickly and went back to the couch to sit. I set on the couch for only about two minutes, when I thought to myself that I should take a shower and get myself prepared to leave. I had planned that I would get a rental car and go around Vegas to find myself a small place to stay. I didn't feel very comfortable being at Britney's apartment even though she and Melvin were very welcoming.

I grabbed a set of fresh clothes and headed to the bathroom to take a shower. The bathroom was almost as junky as the rest of the apartment. There were dirty clothes piled behind the bathroom door, toothpaste spit on the mirror over the sink, and lots of different toiletries on the counter. Next to the toilet was a laundry basket with a stack of magazines inside. When I pulled back the shower curtain, I was disgusted to see so much dirt and soap scum in the tub. I ran the water and got in any way. As I began to shower I felt a bit dizzy. I knew that the medication was starting to kick in. Suddenly from the other side of the curtain I can hear the bathroom door open. "Tyler", Melvin called out to me. "Hey Melvin, I'll be out in a sec", I quickly replied. "Oh, no worries. I just got to piss", he said as he flipped open the toilet lid and began to pee. He peed for what seemed like five minutes as I awkwardly stood in the shower waiting for him to finish. "Hope you don't mind, I walk around naked while I'm home alone", he said from the other side of the curtain. "This is your home bro. You are the king of your castle. Thanks for giving me the heads up. I will be out of your hair in a little while. I'm going around to find me a place today", I said. "Cool. So I figured out where I know you from", he said as he pulled back the shower curtain, holding a copy of The Doll House magazine that I was in. I was shocked that he pulled back the curtain but I tried to play it cool. "Oh, yes man, that's me", I said nervously. "I'm sorry bro, if I'm making you feel uncomfortable", he said as he continued to hold the magazine. I continued to shower trying to stop my eyes from looking down at his privates. I honestly hoped he was completely straight because I wasn't in the mood for any funny business. "Oh, you're good bro", I said, but I didn't mean it. "So are you just a model", he asked as he closed the shower curtain. "Yes I am. I actually came back to Vegas to do more modeling work", I said. "Well that's awesome bro. I'm going back to bed. We'll talk more about it later", he said as he closed the bathroom door. My heart pounded nervously as I felt the hydrocodone taking over me. I got out of the shower, put on my clothes and went back to the couch. I laid back and began to doze off. Even though I wasn't comfortable at Britney's house, I felt really good. My body was totally relaxed and I felt high. I felt like I could just get up and fly. I figured I would lay there for a couple more hours until my high wore off.

The next thing I knew was my phone ringing at 11:47am, and it was Britney. She was asking me if I had left her apartment yet and wanted to make sure I was okay. I told her everything was fine and that I was just about to leave. After I hung up with her I quickly called a cab and started to gather my things. When the cab came I went to rent myself a car.

TYLER IV

Since I had saved my money from the modeling gigs that I had done months ago, I knew that I could find a small apartment that I could afford for a couple of months. I did just that. I found an apartment that was about 10 minutes from the Las Vegas Strip. It wasn't in the cleanest neighborhood but I knew it was only temporary. I went to a nearby department store and bought an air mattress, along with a few other household things to make my stay comfortable.

Throughout my first night in my apartment, the pain in my leg and ankle had gotten really bad. I took three of my prescribed pills to help ease the pain. Taking those pills made me to feel very good. I felt free within my own life as the pills ran their course. I had quickly gotten to a point; where I would pop another pill whenever I felt my high coming down. I constantly reassured myself that I wasn't becoming addicted to the medication. After about three straight days of sleeping and constantly taking my pills, I had begun to feel like I was getting off track with my plans of making money. Since modeling had become a life for me, I decided to get back into that. I felt like I already knew quite a bit about the business. Now that I actually had national exposure, I could go to any agency to get more work. I contacted the biggest talent and modeling agency I could find in the Las Vegas area, and that was Levitt.

The Levitt Agency wasn't as popular as The Trusey Agency, but it wasn't too far behind. Levitt was an agency ran by twin brothers Jason and John Levitt. They were once print and television child stars back in the early 70's. They were very famously known for their roles in the "Krazy Krunchin' Kites" cereal commercials. Now, they were of course older, and running their own agency. Instead of calling first, I felt like I should just show up at their office, which was about 20 minutes outside of the downtown Las Vegas area.

Before I got to their office I stopped at a print shop to print out several of my photos to present to them. When I got to their office, I was greeted by their receptionist, whom from a first glance I thought was Amanda. When I saw her, my heart froze for about five seconds. Her name was Kristina, though I gave her my name, and told her I had an appointment with John. I was lying, but I knew they wouldn't just turn me away. She looked through her appointment book and couldn't find my appointment, of course. Feeling a little unorganized, she apologized and asked me to have a seat while she went to get him. Before she walked away, I handed her one of my prints, "this is to refresh his memory, just in case he has forgotten me", I said giving her a wink. I sat down and waited for about a minute.

John came out of his office with a puzzled look on his face holding my picture. "Tyler", he asked. "Yes sir", I said standing up to shake his hand. "Thanks for stopping by" he said. I can tell he really didn't know me, but pretended to. He was too embarrassed to have possibly forgotten me. "Follow me", he said as he took me to his office down the hall. "So are you a model looking for work", he asked as he sat behind his desk. I set in the chair right across from his desk. "Yes, I've done a lot of work already. I've been in magazines and a few other things", I said as I pulled out my printed photos, laying them in front of him on his desk. "These are really nice photos", he said as he scanned them. "Thanks, I'm easy to work with and I work very hard", I said nodding. "Yes, you and every other model", he said as he looked up at me. "How long have you had that scar on your face", he asked drily. Suddenly, I felt like he knew everything. I felt like he was about to read straight through my game. "Oh, this scar is recent. I was walking up the stairs at my apartment and slipped and hit my face on a sharp railing", I lied. "You got to be careful, you're a model", he said as he began to laugh and look back down at the pictures. "Which agency were you signed with to get these shots", he asked. I really couldn't lie about this one because "The Trusey Agency's" logo was at the bottom of a couple of the photos. "The Trusey Aganecy", I said. "Oh, you were signed to Mark", he asked surprised. I nodded and said yes. "That's an old friend of mine and my brother. We go far back. What happened with you working with Mark", he asked. My heart began to beat hard. I had to think very fast. "Oh, nothing. I was signed to Mark when I lived in Atlanta. I moved back here to Vegas to take care of my dying mother. I knew that I wouldn't be able to work as much as I had wanted, being away from Atlanta. Even though he does business all over the country, we both agreed to terminate my contract", I said with a straight face. "Wow, that' impressive to be featured in The Doll House... Well I'll be honest with you, my brother and I will not sign any model that has been previously signed to Mark Trusey or any other agency that we do business with. There will be a huge conflict that we aren't willing to risk our professional bonds over. However, off the record, if you are truly wanting to work and make some money, I can work with you on other business", he said as he comfortably leaned back in his chair. "At this point my mom is sick and I really need to make some cash", I said desperately. "Hmmm... Okay... My brother and I have a fashion show to attend this Saturday for a new fashion line. Are you busy that day", he asked slowly. "No I'm free", I said quickly. "Wear a nice suit. I believe I have some clients that can definitely use your work. Here, write down your contact info, and I'll be in touch with you tomorrow with the address of the venue", he said as he handed me a pen and yellow sticky note to write on. "Yes, sure. Whatever you need I got you", I said feeling excited.

After my meeting with John I felt great. I didn't know what type of work he was going to get me but I was excited to be considered. I know I lied but I felt like I had to. There had been far too much going on in my life and I just couldn't face the truth of it all. I had become obsessed with the thought of making money. I just couldn't bear the thought of going back to nothing. I had considered selling drugs and getting into other illegal practices but I didn't want the stress of running from the law and possibly ending up back in jail.

Even though it was only Wednesday, later that evening I went out to find a nice suit to wear for that weekend. I found the perfect suit that was a little over a thousand dollars. Sure, I could have found something cheaper, but I wanted to make a stronger serious impression. I figured that I would return the suit back to the store in about a week for a full refund. The suit was a light grey, slim fitted three piece suit. I even bought new shoes to match it.

TYLER V

The next evening I received a call from John. He gave me the address to the venue which was actually at the Ritz-Carlton hotel and told me the event was going to take place on Saturday, around 8pm. He told me that he would put my name on the guest list and again, to wear a suit.

Later that night, my ankle was in pain, so I decided to take my medication. Even though the pain wasn't all that severe I just felt like I needed it. Since the next day was Friday, and I didn't have anything to do until Saturday, I decided to take three pills. I knew taking that much was a bit extreme but I loved how these pills made me feel. I felt higher than high, and it was legal. I was able to forget all the mess that my life had become. Nothing mattered when I had those pills in my system.

The next day I woke up in the late afternoon. I felt like I had a slight hangover. When I got up from my blow-up mattress I felt like I was hovering. I couldn't feel myself touching the floor. I laughed to myself because I figured that I was still high.

The Boy X Chronicles

I went to the kitchen and fixed myself a ham sandwich and took two more pills. I just didn't seem to care, even though there was a small voice inside telling me not to. That same voice was way too small to compete with the over grown monster, that also resided inside of me.

Eventually I dosed off again. When I woke up it was dark outside. I looked at the time on my phone and seen that it said "Saturday 12:34 am". In my mind at that time, I thought I had just missed the entire event. I thought I slept the entire Saturday night away. I was confused and began to panic. I went through my phone and searched for John's number. I had begun to text him and tell him how sorry I was for missing the event. I went on to tell him that my mother had actually died. Before I hit the send button, I set and thought for a brief moment and realized that "Saturday 12:34 am", was the start of the day not the end. I felt crazy and in raged. I grabbed my bottle of pills and ran into the bathroom. I stood over the toilet and opened the bottle and began to pour them in, but I couldn't. I flushed the toilet and watched the water swirl into the drainage. Every particle of water represented some point in my own life. I've been flushing myself down the drain and I refused to lose this time. I closed the bottle of pills and set them on the counter. I lay down on my mattress and gazed at the ceiling until I dosed off.

The next day I woke up around noon. I spent the entire day prepping myself for that night's event. I went out and found a barber shop nearby to get a clean haircut and shave. I felt like this night could definitely be the start of something new for me. I still didn't know exactly what John had in mind for me but whatever it was, I was going to make the best of it and use it as a leverage to get me to the next level.

TYLER VI

When I arrived early to the event that night, I just didn't want to miss anything. I drove up to the front entrance of the hotel to valet my rental car. I walked inside of the lobby where I gave my name to the guy standing at a podium. He looked through his book, found my name and pointed me down the hall where the event was taking place.

When I walked inside of this large room, there were already a lot of people there enjoying cocktails and talking. At the front of the room was a larger stage and runway aisle. There was a DJ on the side of the stage playing what sounded to me to be trance music. I scanned the room to see if I could see John, but there was no sign of him. I decided to grab myself a cocktail and hangout near the entrance. As I looked around the room I felt overwhelmed with the power and wealth within it. Most of the people here were millionaires that ran their own businesses. They were all dressed elegantly, with the women wearing blinding diamonds. I felt like I was definitely in the right place. I decided that I would walk around and mingle with the people.

Just as I decided to walk around, John enters the room with a woman on his arm, in which I assumed was his wife. John had on an all black tux, while she wore an elegant red gown with pearls. I walked over to him from behind. I tapped him on the back of his shoulder and as he turned in my direction, I reached out my hand to shake his hand. "Hey, how's it going", I said excitedly. "Hey… Do I know you", he asked looking puzzled. "Yes, I'm Tyler. I met with you just the other day", I said smiling. "Tyler, how's it going", another voice said behind me. I turned to look to see that it was John. "Oh wow, I'm sorry. I thought he was you and you were he…", I said stuttering. "It's alright. After 40 plus years it still happens", John said. Jason and his wife looked a bit confused. "Jason, this is Tyler. Tyler this is my brother Jason… Tyler worked for Mark Trusey. He's been featured in a few magazines including The Doll House", John said. "Oh wow, nice. Well Tyler this is my wife Cindy", Jason said as Cindy reached out her hand to me. I shook her hand as she gave me a strange seductive look. Feeling a bit uncomfortable I just smiled and nodded. "Nice to meet you" I said. "Hmm Mmm", she nodded still giving me that look. "Hey Tyler follow me there's some people I would like you to meet", John said. "Nice meeting you both", I said as I began to walk away from Jason and his wife.

"My brother could be a bit strange at times", John said as we walked through the crowd. "He seemed fine to me", I laughed.

"I'm going to get straight to it. I'm sure you've been probably wondering why I invited you here… I'm not sure how you may feel about this. There's a lot of money you can make… Outside of running the agency with my brother I also run an escorting company. This is actually one of my top paying client's event. She's a fashion designer from New York… The pay will be great", John said. I was immediately hesitant. I felt like he could have taken his time to wheel me into the idea. "Escorting? Exactly what would I have to do…", I asked, playing dumb. I have definitely heard of the escorting business and I've even had sex for money before, but it's never been presented to me as a career. "All you'll have to do is spend a little time with her. She may want to have sex, but not necessarily", John said. "How much are we talking", I asked. "I already have two other guys working for me in this business. IF this is something you can't do I will understand", he said. "How much are we talking", I asked again. "Five", he said. In my mind I was thinking that five hundred dollars would be nice. I can easily layup with someone for five hundred a night. I quickly envisioned myself making lots of fast money. "Five hundred", I said. "No, no, no, FIVE THOUSAND", John said with a serious tone and face. "I only take 50%. That still leaves you with $2,500", he said. "Deal", I said before I could think of anything else. "How much work will you be able to get me", I asked. "That depends on you. Your availability. Your likeability. Your flexibility… I know the wealthiest people in Las Vegas and even around this country; from doctors to fast food managers, from government officials to garbage men. I've been doing this type of business with them for many years. When I call you, you'll just have to be ready" he said. "Okay, I'm in. Just let me know…", I said without any hesitation. "You'll make ten times more money than you would as a model. With your looks I can get you lots of business", he said giving me a side eye.

From there, we went on and on just talking about random things when a short chubby lady with loads of makeup, and a huge black curly wig walks up to John. They greeted each other with a kiss on the cheek. As John leaned down to kiss her I heard her ask him, "do you have one for me tonight". Immediately he turned to me and said, "Tyler, I would like for you to meet Vernanda. She's the designer we are here for tonight. Vernanda, this is my newly signed model, Tyler". He gave me a quick awkward wink. I reached out my hand to shake Vernanda's but she pulled me in for a hug. "I don't do handshakes, I do hugs and kisses", she said as she hugged me tightly. "It's a pleasure to meet you and congratulations on your clothing line", I said nervously. "Why thank you. It's nice meeting tall, beautiful, strong men like yourself", she said as she licked and bit her lips giving me the low sexy eye. "Tyler just moved back here to Vegas from Atlanta", John chimed in. "Well that's just wonderful… We'll have plenty of time… I'll see you all later. I have to go and get the fashion show started", she said as slowly walked away, still giving me the low sexy eye. "Oh yeah, she wants you", John laughed. "Yeah,

I see. So what will I have to do with her…", I hesitantly asked. "Whatever she wants. She's a bit kinky… She likes to be fucked hard… Can you handle that", he asked giving me a low uncertain look. "Oh… Okay, fucked hard. Wow… I sure hope so…When was the last time you've spoken to Mark Trusey", I said and asked, randomly changing the subject. I was curious to see if he had spoken to Mark about me at all. If so, I wanted to pick his brain about what Mark may have told him. "Oh, it's been at least a year since I've last heard from Mark. Here take this. It'll be sure to get you in the right mood", he said changing the subject, as he handed me an Ecstasy pill. I looked at the pill for a few seconds. I couldn't believe what was happening. I've done Ecstasy as a teenager but haven't touched it in years. Ecstasy normally puts me on a different type of high. It increases my sexual desires by ten and gives me lots of energy. "Ok, sure. So when will I get paid", I asked. "I will give you half now and the other half after. You can meet me at my office tomorrow and I will give you the rest", he said. "Tomorrow is a Sunday. So you're going to be in your office on a Sunday", I asked. "Tyler, in my business I work every day, all day. My life is my work. I don't have a wife because she is my work", he said as he dug inside his suit jacket pocket and pulled out a small roll of one hundred dollar bills. "Here you go", he said sneaking the money into my hand. I immediately grabbed tight to the money and started to count it. "Wait this is only one thousand dollars", I said. "Whoa, slow down cowboy. That's all I have on me, you'll get the rest tomorrow. I'm a fair business man", he said with a serious face.

Moments later the fashion show had begun. From the looks of things the fashion show was filled with short plus sized women. The clothing line called "Verna", was a line for short plus sized women. The entire time as I watched the fashion show I became extremely nervous. My palms were sweating a bunch and my ankle had begun to hurt a lot. I had wrapped one of my prescribed pills in tissue and put it in my pocket before I left home, just in case this was to happen. I went and grabbed a cocktail from one of the waiters to take my medication. I took my medication and decided to also take the Ecstasy pill. I wasn't sure what affects this will have on me, but I wanted to be out of the pain and hopefully in the mood.

After about 30 minutes, the fashion was done. Vernanda walked through the crowd of people and back over to where John and I were standing. "So how did you like the show and designs", she asked as she approached. "It was wonderful. I really enjoyed every piece I seen", John replied. "Yes so did I", I also replied. "So I will leave now and let you two get a bit more acquainted", John said before he walked away. By this time I was beginning to feel my high from the Ecstasy. I took a deep breath and allowed my mind to get in the mood. "So shall we leave now", she looked at me seductively and asked. "Yes, are we going to your place", I asked. "Yes, I'm actually staying here in the hotel for the night. Room 1826, in thirty minutes. I'll leave the door on the latch for you", she said as she slowly walked away. Even though I didn't find her nearly attractive, the drug inside of me wanted her badly by this point.

After thirty minutes, I left the venue and walked to the lobby of the hotel trying to find the elevators. In the lobby waiting at the Valet Parking counter was Jason and his wife. As I walked past Jason gave me a smile and a nod, while his wife gave me a low seductive sexy eye. I felt like I was in one of those slow motion movie scenes. Her eyes said it all. I can tell she wanted me and honestly, I wanted her too. She was a hot middle aged cougar with bleached blond hair, a new set of breast, slim body, sexy thick lips, with haunting blue grayish eyes. Feeling the way I was at the moment, Jason is lucky to have been standing there with her. If he wasn't; I would have taken her to the Men's room…

When I got up stairs I quickly found Vernanda's room. When I walked in, I can smell her perfume. It was a light rosey scent. "Hello", I called out as I entered the room. "Come on in bonito", Vernanda said. I walked further into the room to find Vernanda in the bed face down with her naked ass in the air. I laughed a bit in the inside at the site. "I want you to fuck me loco, all noche. There are condoms on the desk behind me. Hurry…Papi…"she said seductively. I quickly noticed her way of talking Spanglish. She would slip in a couple Spanish words while speaking English. I quickly took off my clothes and slipped on a condom. Without any hesitation or complications, I penetrated her from behind. "Siiiiii, this is exactly what I need. Give it to me", she moaned. The whole time I couldn't see her face because all the weave from her head was covering it. I could only hear her voice. "Make me tu punto", she yelled to me. After about thirty strong minutes I had reached my climax. "Grab another condom, let's go again", she said. Thankfully I was high on Ecstasy, because in any normal situation I would have been sleep at that point. I grabbed another condom and slipped it on and we went at it again. If having sex with people for money was this easy and profitable, I knew this was going to be something I did for a while. I'm sure I wouldn't want to do it forever but at least until I'm financially where I want to be.

After my session with Veranda, I went down stairs, got into my car and headed home. The whole ride home, I couldn't believe that I had just made so much money in such a little time period. Honestly, just the $1000 was enough to satisfy my desire. It was money but since John was offering more, I wanted even more.

TYLER VII

The next day, the only thing on my mind was to pick up the rest of my money from John. I got myself ready and went down to his office. When I walked up to the glass office door, I could see John sitting in at the receptionist desk on the computer. I grabbed the handle to open the door but it was locked. John looked up and said "We're closed on Sundays". I knocked on the glass door looking confused as he got up to unlock and open the door. "Hey, you're Tyler right", he said as he opened the door. It then dawned on me that this wasn't John but Jason. Most twins usually have a slight difference to where you could tell them apart but not John and Jason. They were the same height, same build, same haircut, same smile, same voice, it was haunting. "Yes, I'm here to meet with John", I said confused. "Hey, John. Someone is here to see you", he yelled to the back at John.

Moments later John came out of his office. "Tyler, come on back to my office", John said when he seen that it was me. Jason had a strange look on his face as if he was curious about

142

my presence. I followed John back to his office. "So how was your first night on the job", he asked as he took his seat behind his desk. "It was adventurous. Very different but I'm ready for more work", I said. "Nice, because I have more work for you this coming weekend", John said as he pulled out a stack of one hundred dollar bills from his desk drawer. "So where's the work this weekend", I asked. "It's a married middle aged woman and her husband is going out of town. She's going to meet you at the Marriott Hotel on Saturday evening. She's one of my regular clients. I've already shown her your pictures. She's a nice one. She really likes young guys", John said as he counted out $1500. "Can I see her pictures? What if I get there and I don't want to have sex with her", I said jokingly. John looked up at me with a serious look and said, "It's your job to be the client's fantasy. It's like customer service. You don't have to like how the customer looks, to give them good service. Besides you have a little extra courage", he said as he slid me a tiny glass bottle of cocaine. My blood rushed to my head quickly. I couldn't believe he was encouraging me to get high on cocaine. For a second I just stared at the tiny bottle.

"Have you booked my flight for Friday yet", Jason asked as he walked into John's office. I quickly grabbed the tiny bottle and hoped that Jason didn't see it. "Yep, you are all booked. Friday, at 12:34 pm, first class to L.A.", John said to Jason. "Okay great. Thanks brother. I'm sorry Tyler, I haven't had a chance to really talk to you the other night", Jason said as he reached to shake my right hand in which I had the bottle of cocaine in. I quickly and awkwardly gave him my left hand to shake instead. "It's okay, I understand. I'm just here trying to get some modeling work", I quickly said without thinking. "Well you said the other night you worked with Mark", Jason began to question. "I was just explaining to him that we don't represent models that has been signed to other agencies that we work with", John quickly chimed in. "Correct. I need to call Mark anyways, I heard one of his models were killed in a car crash in Atlanta", Jason said looking puzzled at John. "Well we were just finishing up any ways. I'll walk you out Tyler", John said. "Oh ok, well good luck to you Tyler. I'm sorry we couldn't help you", Jason added. "No problem, I really do appreciate the consideration", I said as I stood to follow John out. I was so relieved that John quickly changed the subject without any other word or mention of Mark. Jason's curiosity felt thick in the air. I can tell he probably didn't believe in what we were saying.

We walked outside to my car. "So I told you my brother can be a bit weird at times. He knows nothing about my side businesses, so you can't say a word to anyone. As a matter of fact, let's never meet here at my office again, I don't want him to grow suspicious of you being around", John said. "Wow. Okay.. My lips are sealed", I said. "Good. I will be in touch with you during the week", John said as I opened the door to get into the car. "Okay great. I will talk to you soon", I said.

After I left John's office I went to a pharmacy to refill my prescription. Even though my ankle had healed a lot and I could walk on it, it still caused me a great deal of pain at random times. While I was waiting for my medicine to be prepared, I grabbed a copy of "EVERYBODY" magazine and skimmed through some of the pages until I came across a picture of Lance. There was an entire article dedicated to him with a head line that read "Rest In Peace to Trusey's Brightest Star". I quickly closed the magazine and put it back on the shelf. I didn't want to have any memories of Lance. I was trying to deny to myself that I ever knew Lance.

After I received my medication, I grabbed a bite to eat and downed three pills.

Days later, I received a call from John telling me that Vernanda wanted another session with me this week. I of course agreed and did what I was paid to do. The second session was even crazier. This time she tied me up to the bed and whipped me with a leather whip. She wore a black leather mask. The entire time I was holding back from laughing loudly in her face. She looked like a licorice flavored Oompa-Loompa. Thankfully, I had some drugs to help me entertain her fantasies.

 John and I had decided that he will meet at my apartment for him to pay me and to give me more drugs. I told him that I needed more drugs to sustain my high while entertaining clients like Vernanda. He gave me an extra supply of drugs in which I took for work and when I was alone as well.

When John seen my apartment he urged that I move out and move into one of his apartments that he rented. John has three fully furnished apartments spread throughout Vegas, that he rents and uses for his side business. Since a lot of his clients are high profiled people he allows them to use one of his apartments instead of possibly blowing their cover sneaking in and out of hotels. Even though his offer for me to move seemed great, I just didn't want to become that dependent on him. I didn't want to give him any more power over me.

TYLER VIII

When the weekend finally came, John came over that
morning and paid me half the money from the middle-aged
lady that he spoke to me about at his office, which was $2000,
plus giving me more Ecstasy and cocaine. In one week I had
already made close to $5000. I was over whelmed by how
quickly I was getting money. I looked up to John now, he was
like my Jesus.

Before I went to the Marriott, John had already texted me the
clients room number. I popped an Ecstasy and snorted a line
of cocaine before I got out of my car. I had a quick rush of high
flowing through my body. I was now ready for whatever. I
went into the hotel and up to the client's room and knocked
on the door. She opened the door and my heart skipped two
beats when I saw that the client was Jason's wife. I couldn't
believe it, seeing her almost blew my high.

"Shocked", she asked sexually as she grabbed my shirt pulling
me into the room. "Well, yes... I am", I said slowly with a
smile. She only had on a red bra and laced red panties. She

was extremely sexy. I would have had sex with her for free. She led me to sit on the bed and walked over to the small bar and poured herself a glass of champagne. "Want a drink", she asked. "Sure", I said quickly as she quickly downed her drink. She poured me a glass and handed it to me. As I began to drink the champagne, she started to unbuckle my pants. She reached through my underwear, pulled out my dick and proceeded to suck it. Feeling so high and erect I quickly drank my champagne and lay back on the bed. After a few moments I got up and laid her on her back, took off my clothes and her panties and returned the favor.

Moments later, we began to passionately kiss while she's on her back and I'm between her legs. Her hands clinched tight into my back, "you're so fucking sexy. I wanted you the moment I seen you", she said as she proceeded to bite my neck. As her finger nails were gripping into my back I could feel a warm wet sensation on my lower back. Immediately after I began to feel that warm wet sensation I felt another pair of hands wrapping around the back of my waist. Feeling so high I couldn't think to react much to it, so I just stayed focused on Cindy. The pair of hands began to massage my lower back as I felt lips and a tongue on my lower back. Feeling almost uncomfortable I turned my head around to see that it was Jason. Or John? I already couldn't tell them apart on a normal day, and now that I'm high I really couldn't tell. The moment of ecstasy was so high that I wasn't going to blow it by asking which one he was. "Do you mind if I join" Jason or John whispered. "Have it your way", I slowly said. He joined in on the sexual experience without any hesitation. We both took turns pleasing the insides of Cindy. This was the best sex I had ever had in my life. This experience was something that I permanently stamped into my memory and would use it to please myself.

After the session I grabbed my clothes and proceeded to put them on. Cindy went into the shower. "I usually don't join in but she's a special kind of client", Jason or John said as he handed me a roll of cash. I then knew that it of course had to be John. "Yes, I see. You scared me for a second, I didn't know who you were. I thought you were...", I said. "My brother? No, no, no he'd kill... all of us", he laughed. "Yeah I bet" I said jokingly but seriously. "You can go ahead and leave. I'm going to stay here for a bit longer. I'll be in touch with you tomorrow. Good work by the way", he said as he put on his clothes. "Thanks", I said as I walked out of the hotel room.

When I got into my car I felt like I had just robbed a bank. My adrenaline was still pumping hard. I couldn't believe that I just had sex with Jason's wife and got paid for it. Even more I couldn't believe that she was having an affair with John. It seemed a bit creepy to me, to cheat on your mate with their twin. It's kind of like doing the same person. I couldn't care much or complain now. I was getting paid to be a toy in their escapade. I would just play along and make my money.

Over the next three weeks, I had made more money than I had made in the past two years combined. I've pleased many different types of clients from; 65 year old men wanting me to please their wives while they sat and watched, to politicians, to priest. I had even started to take this job extremely serious. Meanwhile, my ankle had completely healed and I went to get a membership at a nearby gym. I made sure to maintain my body so that I stayed appealing to my clients. I figured the better I looked the more my demand will go up, and the more money I would make.

Since I was making lots of money I decided to fully furnish my apartment. I took my rental car back and bought myself a BMW that was several years old, but very clean. I was going to move out of my apartment to something a bit upscale but I had grown comfortable where I was. Even though the neighborhood wasn't the greatest, it had become home to me. It fit my cold, dark demeanor. I had become friends with a cocaine dealer that went by the name of Red. He lived in my apartment complex. Red, always hooked me up with extra pills and cocaine whenever I asked. With my own prescription, my supply that was provided by John, and the supply I was buying from Red, I stayed high at all times. I had become reliant on drugs to keep me busy. I never thought that I would be anywhere near addicted to any drug but it was happening.

One day while I was home just watching a television show called "Cheaters", I got an idea to make more money. This show was about someone who feels like their mate is cheating. They hire a team of investigators to set up cameras, to possibly catch their mates cheating. I thought of a plan to buy a very small camera and wear it while I was with a client. I would take the footage and use it to blackmail them. Since some of clients that I have dealt with were public figures, I knew it wouldn't be so hard.

I went out to a cool electronic store and found a small camera hidden inside a pair of sunglasses. This was going to be perfect to keep everything discreet. The glasses were a jet black regular looking pair of glasses, with the camera hidden in the bridge on the glasses that connected the two lenses.

To test out my plan, I decide to test it out on the priest. By this time I had had at least four appointments with the priest within the last three weeks. Usually when I have a session with a client, I'm not always aware of exactly who they are. The only reason why I knew this guy was a priest is because I've actually seen him on television. His actual name was Roger Ferguson, even though he told me his name was Steve. He was about 55 years old and in really good shape. He was very well known in Las Vegas. The people and his followers loved him. Even though he would pay for my services he always tipped me more and more each time. He probably really liked me but I had no emotional attachment to any of my clients. I was all about the money.

John called me on a Thursday and told me that the Priest wanted an appointment with me that evening at 5, at our usual place which was at one of John's apartments. I arrived at the apartment about thirty minutes before he had arrived. I had set up my small sunglass camera on a shelf directly in front of the bed. On the shelf were a huge flat screen TV, a clock, and several different books. I thought, my sunglasses wouldn't seem so out of place on top of the shelf.

Whenever I would meet up with the priest he always wanted to have a versatile session. This is where he would be the top and switch and be bottom, in which cost him double. He loved to give head. He would spend a good thirty minutes giving me head.

This session was just like any other. The only difference is that this time, it was documented. When I got home that night, I immediately uploaded the footage I had captured from my session with the priest to my tablet. After watching the footage I almost decided not to go through with my plan but the more I thought about how much money I could possibly get, the more I pressured myself to do it.

I schemed up the perfect way to blackmail the priest. I decided to upload the footage privately to YouTube. Since the footage was private, it was only visible to those who had the direct link to the footage. I decided to go to an open confessional at his church one night. Before I got out of my car

I snorted a couple lines of cocaine to give me the edge I needed to pull off my plan. Boldly, I walked into the confessional booth and without saying a word I had begun to play the footage on my phone. The booth was split into two sides; I sat in one side and he sat in the other. We were only separated by a wall made of wood, with a wooden mesh like screen, where we could just barely see each other. I placed my phone's screen up to the side where he was seated, so that he could see it. I had cued the footage up to the point where he was giving me head. The confessional box was consumed with my groans, and a slurping noise he made as he sucked me off. After about five seconds of pure silence he finally spoke. "What do you want from me", he nervously asked. "Everything you got", I replied without contemplating my response. I felt like the devil himself. "Anything you want, just name it", he stuttered from the other side of the booth. "You can make me and all of this go away, for $10,000", I replied devilishly. I felt his soul crumbling from the other side of the booth. His complete silence between speaking reassured me that I had him where I wanted. "Ok, $10,000, I will have it for you in cash tomorrow", he said. "A week. I want $10,000 every week until I say stop", I said forcefully. It felt like I wasn't speaking for myself. Every thought I had just seemed to find its way to the tip of my tongue. "No no no... I can't do that...", he started to say. "Don't tell me what you CAN'T do. I will expose you to everyone. You brought this on yourself. You preach a nice sermon about people just like you. Nasty, dirty, rotten old men that play with little boys. Do as I say or kiss your GOOD life, good bye", I said. "Ok, ok whatever you want", he said. "Meet me tomorrow at 4pm at our usual place with my money. I'm warning you not to try anything funny, and don't have me come looking for you. I will make this video public the day you miss a payment", I said as I left the confession booth. I didn't even wait for him to reply. I wanted him to know I meant business and I was sure my point was clear.

TYLER IX

The next day, I went out to the apartment where I normally met up with the priest, about 45 minutes early. My plan was, just to wait on him to get there to show him that I was serious. Surprisingly, he was there in the parking lot already waiting for me. I pulled up next to him and exited my car. I walked over to his passenger side and before I could reach the door, I could hear the doors unlock. I opened the door and set in the passenger seat, "where's the money", I said boldly. He reached in the back seat behind me and pulled up a small blue duffle bag with his church's name and address printed on it. "Look, I don't think I can afford $10,000 a week. I can't take so much cash out of my bank accounts without it looking suspicious. Is there anything else I could do? I just want this to go away", he asked as I looked through the duffel bag. I honestly could not believe that he was willing to pay me this much money. He was scared and feared ever possibility of that footage ever going public. I smelled his fear and began to love it. The power I felt from this priest was something I never thought I was capable of possessing. I was going to make him

The Boy X Chronicles

pay for the priest that molested me as a child, which I felt began the downward spiral in my life. Here's this "faithful" man of God that prays to God, and now he's praying to me. Sad, so sad but I didn't give a damn, he deserved it. "I want what I want. You have my money here next week, same time. I'll think about letting this whole thing go for only... a million dollars", I said. I know if I left him with a glimmer of hope, he would become hopeful and think that there was a way to get rid of me.

To bring even more fear to his heart, I decided to go to his church that following Sunday and sit as close to the front row as I could. When he noticed my presence his entire demeanor changed. His face turned a bright red as he stuttered through the sermon. I knew I had him right where I wanted.

In between my dealings with the priest, John was still booking me appointments with other clients. I've actually also had been with Cindy and him a few other times. While I wanted to start blackmailing other very wealthy clients, I felt like none of them would be as beneficial to me as the priest. He had a public image that people marveled after. Blackmailing the other clients could possibly get too nasty and somehow back fire...

What if I blackmailed John? But how? Ha, what if I blackmailed Cindy? They wouldn't want Jason to find out that they've sleeping around. The more I thought of this ill plan, the more I seen it working into my favor. I will have to wait for John to bring it up, because if I did, it would seem way too suspicious

TYLER X

The next week my opportunity came. John asked me to meet with Cindy at the same hotel from before. I had begun to wonder why we never met up with Cindy at one of John's apartments. I figured that Jason had no knowledge of these apartments and to keep it better hidden, Cindy didn't either. I guess he didn't want to ruin the risk of Cindy somehow bringing them up at all.

When I walked into the room the scent of warm tropical perfumes intoxicated my nose. I took my shades off and pressed record. I set them on the TV stand, pointing at the bed. "I'll be out in just a moment", Cindy said as she poked her head from the bathroom door. Moments later the room door opened and it's of course John. "Where's the Misses", he asked as he looked around the room. "I just finished my shower", Cindy replied from the bathroom. "You got a hit", I asked John as he walked over to the bed to have a seat. Even though I had already snorted a line before I got out of my car, I craved more. "Sure thing. This have to be the last time we're doing this. I think my brothers getting a bit suspicious", John whispered to me as he handed me a small clear tube of cocaine. "What makes you think that", I asked. "I know my brother. His energy towards me had been a little off. Plus, he randomly asked me; when was the last time I've seen Cindy", he continued to whisper. "Where's he now", I asked him in a whisper. "He's out of town for business. He does a lot of scouting for the agency in other cities", he said. At that moment Cindy walked out of the bathroom in a silky black robe, with a half empty glass of champagne. "Looks like somebody got started early", John said as he took the glass of champagne from Cindy's hand giving her a wet nasty kiss. The passion between the two of them was something that I've never seen before. Even though what they were doing was wrong, I would think they were actually married by the way they showed affection to each other. From there our session began and my sunglasses recorded it all.

As soon as I got home that night I privately uploaded the footage to YouTube.

Several days later, was my third meeting with the priest. I met him in the parking lot of John's apartment at the same time we usually meet, 4pm. I got out of the car and went over to his passenger side as usual. When I got into the car I did notice that this time he had the duffle bag sitting on his lap, instead of the back seat. I set in the car and closed the door. "I've told you before that I can't afford this", he started to say as I cut him off. "I don't want to hear that. I told you...", I said as I grabbed the duffle bag from his lap. Under the duffle bag he held a pistol in his right hand. He quickly raised the gun and shot it. Everything happened so quickly. The shot was so loud and traumatizing that I felt like I was shot. I quickly patted myself down to make sure I was still alive. He looked at me in a bit of shock, but regretful that I didn't die quickly. I can tell he's never shot anything or anyone. We both looked at the dashboard of the car to see a small hole, where the bullet penetrated. In the same moment and breath, I quickly reached for the gun trying to get it from his hands. I was able to give him two quick strong head butts that weaken his grip of the gun. As soon as the gun was in my hand I pointed directly at his forehead and quickly pulled the trigger twice. Two shots rang out so loudly that I went deaf. A loud high pitched buzz rang through my ears. I sat in shock for a couple seconds just looking at his lifeless body. His eyes were still open looking directly at me. The look in his eyes was haunting, and I knew they would be a sight I will never forget. Without thinking I quickly got out of the car and back into my car. I rushed away from the scene with the gun riding in my lap. I was so nervous that I couldn't think straight. The only thing I could think was to go home.

When I arrived home, I ran to my bedroom and placed the gun under my pillow. I paced my apartment, breathing hard trying to think of my next move. I went into my stash of drugs and began to indulge. I didn't care if I overdosed at that time; I just wanted this moment in my life to go away. If I had to die to get rid of this feeling of being a murderer, I was willing. As much hate I had in my heart prior to shooting the priest, I now was feeling regretful. I went to my living room and laid back on the couch, preparing for death to come for me.

The next thing I knew was hearing my cell phone ring, and a thunderous loud knocking at my door. I looked at my phone to see that it was John calling and the time was 3:43 AM. I quickly answered my phone. "Open the door", John said as soon as I answered. In a panic but still high I rushed to the door to open it. "What in the fuck did you do", he asked as he rushed into my apartment. For a brief moment I was dumb founded, I was so high that I actually had forgotten what had occurred earlier that day. "What are you talking about", I asked him. He grabbed me by my neck and rushed me down to the floor. "So, you're going to play fucking stupid", he said as he continued to choke me, as I'm on my back. He knelled over me with a look in his eyes that I've never seen. I couldn't breathe to talk and I just knew he was going to choke me to sleep. Seconds later he released me. "Get the fuck up. You killed Steve...", he yelled. "Steve? Who is Steve", I cried while holding my neck. "Roger Ferguson. The priest. Don't fucking play stupid", he screamed. I took that opportunity to stand to my feet. I felt like John was mad enough to kill me. "They found his body outside of my apartment, tonight. I'm not going down for you. You're going to turn yourself in", he yelled at me. The more he yelled the faster my high was

coming down. My thoughts were starting to come back. "No...
I will not", I began to chuckle as I pulled out my cell phone. I
quickly turned it on and shuffled to the footage of him, Cindy
and me. I cued it to the middle and pressed play. It began to
play at a part where Cindy is moaning. I held up my phone so
he could see. He glanced at the screen and quickly grabbed my
phone from my hand, as he attempted to choke me again. I
was able to get away and run into my bedroom. He threw my
phone against the wall and it shattered into pieces. I quickly
grabbed the gun from under my pillow. I pointed it at him.
"No worries. It's already online... Now you're going to get the
fuck out of here or I'm going to kill your ass like I did Steve", I
said devilishly. He stood with both his hands above his head.
"Please. Please.. Please, don't shot me. Let's think of a way to
make this all go away. I know some great attorneys that will
make this all go away", he begged. "Get the fuck out, now", I
said emotionlessly, as I looked him dead in the eyes. "Please
don't shot me", he repeated over and over again as I followed
him to my front door.

When he got to the door he ran out quickly as if I was going to
chase after him. I watched outside my apartment's window as
he got into his car and sped off. My high was definitely coming
down fast and the paranoia had started to really sink in. I ran
back to my room and put the gun back under my pillow. I felt
like I couldn't stay at my apartment because I wasn't sure if
John was going to call the police or not.

I decided to leave and go to Britney and Melvin's apartment. Even though it was so late I was hoping that maybe Melvin was still up watching television. Since John had broken my phone there was no way for me to call before I arrived. I sort of felt bad because I haven't spoken to Britney in months, since the last time I was at her apartment. When I arrived at their door I knocked quietly. I seen from the other side of their peep hole the flickering light from the television which meant it was on. I could also see that someone was looking through the peep hole. The door opened and it was Melvin in nothing but his red boxer short underwear. "Aye, bro. What are you doing here so late? Are you okay? What happened to your neck", he asked me quietly. "Yes, I'm fine. I'm sorry to come here so late, is Britney awake", I asked desperately as I rubbed my hands on my neck. I didn't see until later that John had left multiple bruises on my neck from choking me half to death. "No she's asleep but you're welcome to come in. She has to be up for work in a couple hours", he said. "Thanks a lot", I said as I walked in and set on the couch.

As I set down I noticed that Melvin was watching porn but it was on mute. "Excuse me. I like to watch a little porn before I go to bed", he slightly chuckled as he sat next to me on the couch. "Oh it's fine man, it's your house, do as you please", I said. At that point I had started to question myself on why I even thought to come over here. I was so paranoid that I wasn't thinking straight. "Were you in a fight or something?

You look pretty beat up", Melvin chuckled. "Yea just a little scuffle with some guy", I shrugged off.

The longer I set there the more I wanted to leave. This situation was way too awkward. Here I am at my ex-girlfriend's house, watching porn with her boyfriend after I killed a man. Today had been such a crazy day; I just wanted it all to end. As I set there I started to think of another plan. I decided then that I will leave town tomorrow and head to Los Angeles. Even though I didn't know anyone from Los Angeles, I figured I just needed to get away, fast. As I set replaying all that happened in my head, I remembered that I left the gun at my apartment. I knew will have to go back to my apartment in the morning to retrieve the gun, from under my pillow. That was the only evidence they could use against me. Thinking back, I wished that I would have gotten rid of the gun right after I shot him. As I set there planning my escape from Las Vegas I surprisingly dozed off to sleep.

The next morning, I was woken up by Melvin pouring a bowl of cereal. I lay on the couch with my eyes closed. I could hear Melvin's footsteps getting closer. I could also hear that he had picked up the television remote from the coffee table, in front of the couch. I opened my eyes to see Melvin's naked ass several inches from my face, as he stood in front of me with the remote turning the television on. I quickly closed my eyes. As he flipped through the channels, I can hear that he stopped on the news. "Priest Roger Ferguson, found shot to death in his car last night", the news anchors begins to say as I quickly rose from the couch. "Hey bro, good morning", Melvin said as he turned to see me awake. "Hey... Thanks for letting me stay. I have to go", I said quickly and awkwardly. "Are you sure you're okay? You're acting strange bro, like you've killed a man or something", Melvin jokingly laughed. "No, I just have some very important business I have to take care of this morning", I said as I opened the door to walk out. That was the most awkward exit I have ever made in my life.

I got into my car and quickly headed to my apartment. Just as I planned, I wanted to retrieve the gun and dispose of it before I skipped town. When I got to my apartment everything felt peaceful inside, even though John and I had a scuffle the night before. I went into my room and grabbed the gun and put it inside one of the small duffle bags, that was still filled with cash that I had received from the priest a couple weeks ago. I didn't bother to grab any pieces of furniture or clothes; I wanted to get out of there as fast as I could. Suddenly, there was a knock on the door. Feeling extremely nervous, I quietly walked to the door to look out of the peep hole. It was Red, so I opened the door quickly. "Hey bro, what's up", I said as I opened the door. It wasn't unusual for Red to show up at my door, so I didn't think anything was suspicious about it. "I just wanted to make sure you were home. I got some new shit that will knock you off your feet. I'll have it a little later on today. How long are you going to be home", he asked in a stutter. I felt like his demeanor was a bit strange, but I played it cool. He has never told me that he would have something later that day; he always came to me with the supply. Now, it seemed like he was up to something. "I'm actually getting ready to head to the store in a few moments", I lied. I wanted to throw him off, since I wasn't sure exactly what his purpose was. "Okay cool, I'll just see you later", he said as he walked away. I closed the door and thought for a moment that I was just over reacting and over thinking.

When I walked out of my apartment, I looked around to see if I could see anything that may have seen out of place. I got to my car and started it up and just as I was about to put the car in gear a police car drives and stops directly in front of me, blocking me in. Two policemen jumped out of the car with their guns drawn, "get out of the vehicle with your hands up", the police yelled to me. Feeling so overwhelmed with fear I followed their instructions.

As I got out of the car there were two more police cars pulling up to the scene. They all surrounded my car. I held my hands high as the two police officers forcefully threw me to the ground and hand cuffed me. "You are being charged with murder", one of the officers said as he began to read me my rights. When they picked me off the ground, I looked back to see that they had found the gun inside the duffle bag. There was so much going on that I went deaf, temporarily. I felt like I couldn't hear or comprehend anything that was going on. I was just existing. I was caught. The gun was found with me. I knew I was going to prison for a very long time. My life, once again crumbled and repeated its' unforgiving cycle. They put me in the back of the police car and began to drive away. As we were leaving my apartment complex's parking lot, I noticed John sitting in his car, watching as they took me to jail. I knew then that he snitched me out. Seeing him there really lit my heart on fire, I wished I had killed him the night before when I had a chance to. All I could see now was red and I wanted him to hurt. I hoped he truly enjoyed the sight of them taking me to jail because his hell was just about to start...

The Boy X Chronicles

THE BOY CHRONICLES

Acknowledgements

Thank you God for life and giving me a new endeavor to pursue, which is writing. This book was literally written all around the world. Yep, even in Antarctica. Thank you for taking your time to read this story. For the many people that has read and supported Reason Why I Sing; I greatly appreciate your love and dedication to that project. A VERY SPECIAL THANKS to my BIG COUSIN MONA SPEARS. You have no idea on how much you've encouraged me to continue to write and publish my stories. I thank God for you CUZ! Many others also helped in the process and I greatly appreciate your help and encouragement. It's not easy to stay motivated in today's time but you all have kept me focused. To the love of my life (myself, my soul/spirit), I am EXTREMELY proud of you. Your courage, through all you've been through in life speaks volumes. I thank God for you the most. You could have been anybody else but you've chosen to be ME. Thanks! Love Y'all!

Be sure to follow me on Instagram.com/itsmikespears

itsMikeSpears.com

BE SURE TO CHECK OUT OTHER TITLES BY MIKE SPEARS

MIKE SPEARS

REASON WHY I SING

Reason Why I Sing is a cautionary tale of Mike Spears's experiences as an artist for a major recording label and his journey through the dark side of the music industry. Names, companies, and other details have been changed in the story to protect the privacy of those involved, but the stories documented are all based on real-life events.

Mike details his humble beginnings in small-town Illinois and his journey to Atlanta, a major music city that has produced some of the biggest stars of R&B and other genres. During his time as a signed artist, Mike recalls dealing with sexual manipulation, betrayal, and loss. He writes about losing himself and his values on the way to stardom, as well as his path back to being true to himself and his art.

"I am exposing a lot about myself. I become completely naked and allow my flaws to show in this story. I've lived a life where I have pretended to be more than I was, till one day I was sick of myself. I had grown annoyed with who I was because it was fake and lacking substance," says Spears of those days.

For More Info On Mike Spears visit:
www.itsmikespears.com

SPEARIT
PUBLISHING

Stay in touch with me:

www.itsmikespears.com

instagram.com/itsMikeSpears
twitter.com/itsMikeSpears

BE YOU, BE FREE.

-Mike Spears

www.ingramcontent.com/pod-product-compliance
Lightning Source LLC
Chambersburg PA
CBHW060057150626
46556CB00017BA/1118